AMY ZHANG

Falling into Place

GREENWILLOW BOOKS
An Imprint of HarperCollins*Publishers*

Thanks first and foremost to my editor, Virginia Duncan, for making all of my crazy dreams come true. To Preeti Chhibber, Gina Rizzo, Tim Smith, and the rest of the Greenwillow team, whose dedication and enthusiasm for this book never seem to end. To Emily Keyes, for being my agent and fairy godmother and therapist and friend and everything in between. To Matt Roeser, for the gorgeous cover—I still can't stop looking at it. To Mark O'Brien, John Hansen, Ari Susu-Mago, and Olivia Jones, for the briefcase conversation and everything that followed. To all the wonderful teachers in my life: Josh Loppnow, Addie Degenhardt, Debra Kelly, and particularly Justin "Danger" Moore, whose monomyth assignment eventually became this book. To my friends, especially Elodie Huston, Lexi Arenz, and Megan Kapellen, for making me a better person. And to my family, of course, for always believing that I could do anything.

△▽△

Falling into Place

Copyright © 2014 by Amy Zhang

The text of this book is set in 12-point Garamond 3.

Book design by Paul Zakris

Library of Congress Cataloging-in-Publication Data

Zhang, Amy, (date.)

Falling into place / by Amy Zhang.

"Greenwillow Books."   pages cm

Summary: "One cold fall day, high school junior Liz Emerson steers her car into a tree. This haunting and heartbreaking story is told by a surprising and unexpected narrator and unfolds in nonlinear flashbacks even as Liz's friends, foes, and family gather at the hospital and Liz clings to life"—Provided by publisher.

ISBN 978-0-06-229504-0 (hardback)—ISBN 978-0-06-236788-4 (intl. ed.)

[1. Suicidal behavior—Fiction. 2. Emotional problems—Fiction. 3. High schools—Fiction. 4. Schools—Fiction. 5. Interpersonal relations—Fiction. 6. Conduct of life—Fiction. 7. Youths' writings.] I. Title.

PZ7.1.Z42Fal 2014

[Fic]—dc23   2014018247

14 15 16 17 18 LP/RRDH 10 9 8 7 6 5 4 3 2 1

First Edition

 GREENWILLOW BOOKS

To Chris and Sophie,
When I told you I wasn't dedicating this book to you guys, I lied.
Of course this is for you.

LAWS OF MOTION

First Law

A body at rest will remain at rest, and a body in motion will remain in motion with a constant velocity, unless acted upon by a force.

Second Law

Force is equal to the change in momentum (mV) per change in time. For a constant mass, force equals mass times acceleration (F = ma).

Third Law

For every action, there is an equal and opposite reaction.

CHAPTER ONE
Laws of Motion

On the day Liz Emerson tries to die, they had reviewed Newton's Laws of Motion in physics class. Then, after school, she put them into practice by running her Mercedes off the road.

As she lies on the grass with the shattered window tangled in her hair, her blood all around her, she looks up and sees the sky again. She begins to cry, because it's so blue, the sky. So, so blue. It fills her with an odd sadness, because she had forgotten. She had forgotten how very blue it was, and now it is too late.

Inhaling is becoming an exceedingly difficult task. The rush of cars grows farther and farther away, the world blurs at the edges, and Liz is gripped by an inexplicable urge to get to her feet and chase the cars, redefine the world. In this moment, she realizes what death really means. It means that she will never catch them.

Wait, she thinks. *Not yet.*

She still doesn't understand them, Newton's Three Laws of Motion. Inertia and force and mass and gravity and equal and opposite reactions still do not quite fit together in her head, but she is ready to let go. She is ready for it all to end.

It is then, when she releases her need to understand, that everything falls into place.

Things just aren't that simple.

And suddenly it's very clear to her that every action is an interaction, and everything she has ever done has led to something else, and to another something else, and all of that is ending here, at the bottom of the hill by Highway 34, and she is dying.

In that moment, everything *clicks.*

And Liz Emerson closes her eyes.

SNAPSHOT: SKY

We lie on the red-checkered blanket with weeds and flowers all around us, caught in the fleece. Our breaths carry our dandelion wishes higher, higher, until they become the clouds we watch. Sometimes we looked for animals or ice cream cones or angels, but today we only lie there with our palms together and our fingers tangled, and we dream. We wonder what lies beyond.

One day, she will grow up and imagine death as an angel that will lend her wings, so she can find out.

Death, unfortunately, is not in the business of lending wings.

CHAPTER TWO

How to Save a Corpse

I watch the spinning lights close in, wrapping the scene in long lines of ambulances and yellow tape. Sirens wail and paramedics spill out, running and slipping down the great hill in their haste. They surround the Mercedes, crouch beside her, the glass crunching beneath their feet.

"No gag reflex. Get the tube ready, I need RSI intubation—"

"Can you start a line from there? Jaws of life . . . get the fire department!"

"—no, forget that, break the windshield—"

So they do. They remove the glass and carry her up

the hill, and no one notices the boy standing near the mangled bits of her car, watching.

Her name is on his lips.

Then he is pushed back by a policeman, forced back to the crowd of people who have gotten out of their cars to catch a glimpse of the scene, the blood, the body. I look past the circle and see the traffic rapidly piling up in every direction, and right then, it's very easy to imagine Liz somewhere in the long line of cars, sitting inside an intact Mercedes, her hand pressed to the horn, her swearing drowned out by the pounding bass of the radio.

It's impossible. It's impossible to imagine her as anything but alive.

The fact, however, is that the word *alive* no longer accurately describes Liz Emerson. She is being pushed into the back of an ambulance, and for her, the doors are closing.

"She's tachycardic—and hypotensive, can you—"

"I need a splint, she's got a complex fracture in the superior femur—"

"No, just *get the blood stopped*! She's going into shock!"

As everyone moves and rushes around her, a musical of beeping machines and panic, I just watch her, her hands, her face. Her hair falling out of the hasty braid. The foundation across her cheeks, too thin to cover the graying skin.

When I look around, I can see her heart beating on three

different monitors. I can see the steam her breath makes on the mask. But Liz Emerson is not *alive*.

So I lean forward. I place my lips beside her ear and whisper for her to *stay, stay alive*, over and over again. I whisper it as though she'll hear me, like she used to. As though she'll listen.

Stay alive.

CHAPTER THREE
The News

Monica Emerson is on a plane when the hospital calls. Her phone is turned off, and the call goes straight to voicemail.

An hour later, she turns on her phone and listens to her messages as she makes her way to baggage claim. The first is from the marketing division of her company—something about her next trip to Bangkok. The second is from the dry cleaners. The third is silent.

The fourth begins just as she spots her suitcase on the carousel, so the words "Your daughter was in a car accident" don't register right away.

She makes herself listen to the entire thing one more time, breathe, and when it ends and the nightmare doesn't, she turns and runs.

The suitcase takes another turn on the carousel.

Julia is almost halfway through her calculus homework when the phone in the hall rings.

It makes her jump, because no one ever calls her house. She has a cell and her father has three, and Julia has never understood why they needed a landline too.

Regardless, she goes into the hall to answer, because conic parametric equations are giving her a headache.

"Hello?"

"Is this George De—"

"No," she says. "This is Julia. His daughter?"

"Well, this is the emergency contact number we have for Elizabeth Emerson. Is it correct?"

"Liz?" She twirls the phone cord around her fingers and wishes, suddenly, that she had never let Liz put her dad down as an emergency contact. It wasn't like he was ever around for emergencies. *Stupid,* she thought. "Yes, this is the right number. Is Liz—what's going on?"

There's a pause. "Is your father home?"

Julia pushes down her annoyance, chokes it, cinches the phone line tighter around her fingers and watches them turn purple. "No," she says. "Is something wrong? Is Liz okay?"

"I'm not authorized to release the information to anyone except Mr. George Dev—"

"Did something happen to Liz?"

Another hesitation, and then a sigh. "Elizabeth was admitted to St. Bartholomew's Hospital a little while ago. She was in a car accident—"

Julia drops the phone, grabs her car keys, and Googles directions to the hospital on the way to her car.

Kennie is on a bus with the rest of Meridian High's dance team. At the moment the Mercedes flips over, she is leaning over the back of her seat, trying to grab Jenny Vickham's bag of sour gummies while the bus driver yells at her to sit down. She is happy, because soon she'll dance beneath spotlights as the only junior in the front row. Soon they'll win the competition and come back laughing. Soon she'll spin and leap and forget about the baby and the abortion and Kyle and Liz.

I'm happy, she tells herself. *Be happy.*

Both Monica Emerson and Julia are too busy unraveling to remember Kennie. They couldn't have called anyway— Kennie has no phone service on the bus, and her phone is about to die. As Monica and Julia rush for the hospital,

Kennie is traveling in the opposite direction, blissfully ignorant of the fact that her best friend is dying.

She probably won't know for a while. No, she'll come home after winning the competition, cheeks sore from smiling so much, stomach cramped from laughing the whole ride back. She will take a shower and exchange her sparkles and spandex for a worn pair of pajamas. She will sit in the darkness of her room, her wet hair piled atop her head, and scroll through her Facebook feed. She will find it clogged with a story told through statuses, and it will take her breath away.

CHAPTER FOUR

Stay Alive

Liz had planned the crash with an uncharacteristic attention to detail, but not once did St. Bartholomew's Hospital make an appearance in her plans, because she was supposed to die on impact.

She had been excessively careful in choosing the location, however. The highway, the hill, the icy turn, all nearly an hour from her house. She had even driven along the route once, swerved a little, chipped the paint on the Mercedes, for practice. But because she had chosen to crash her car so far away, no one is there to meet her when the ambulance pulls into St. Bartholomew's. No one is there to hold her hand as the doctors wheel her to surgery.

There's only me.

I can only watch.

Stay alive.

I watch the doctors arrive. I watch the flashing scalpels, the eyebrows that curve downward. I watch the hands, the white latex splashed with red.

I watch, and I remember the time Liz fractured her shin in kindergarten playing soccer, already too in love with the sport and already too vain for shin guards, and how we went to Children's Hospital instead of this one. That surgery room had a border of giraffes jumping rope, and Liz had held my hand until the anesthesia pulled her away.

But there are no giraffes jumping rope here, and Liz's hand is broken. This isn't like that surgery, or any of the other ones—the one at Taft Memorial when Liz tore her ACL during a powder puff game, or the one at the dentist's when she'd had her wisdom teeth removed. During those, the doctors had been relaxed. There had been iPod docks in the corners, playing Beethoven or U2 or Maroon 5, and the doctors had seemed . . . well, human.

These surgeons are all hands and knives, cutting and peeling Liz apart, sewing and sewing her back together as though they can trap her soul and lock it away under her skin. I wonder how much of her will be left when they finish.

Stay alive.

But she doesn't want to. She doesn't want to.

I try to remember the last time she was happy, her last good day, and it takes so long to sort through the other memories, the unhappy ones and the empty ones and the shattered ones, that it's easy to understand why she closed her eyes and jerked her wheel to the side.

Because Liz Emerson held so much darkness within her that closing her eyes didn't make much of a difference at all.

CHAPTER FIVE

Five Months Before Liz Emerson Crashed Her Car

On the first Friday of Liz's junior year, only three topics were discussed at lunch: Ms. Harrison's plus-size miniskirt and fishnet stockings, the sheer number of freshman skanks, and the enormous beach party Tyler Rainier was going to throw that night. Over her tray of healthy (by government standards) and inedible (by everyone else's standards) lunch, Liz declared her intentions too. Which meant, of course, that everyone else was going too.

Everyone were the others sitting at the three tables reserved for Meridian High School's elite: the petty, the vain, the jocks, the idiots, the beautiful, the accepted and admired sluts. In particular, her statement was directed at Kennie, who would immediately text Julia—who, due to a scheduling conflict resulting from an overload of AP classes, had a different lunch hour—with the plans.

Liz, Julia, Kennie. That was the way things were, and no one questioned it anymore.

After school, Liz drove home with the radio blasting. She was more lenient on the gas pedal than usual, because she knew she would return to an empty house. Her mom was either in Ohio or Bulgaria that weekend—she couldn't remember. It didn't matter. There was always a business trip, and always another one.

Once upon a time, Liz had loved that her mother traveled. It was like magic, like a fairy tale, to have a mother who crossed oceans and knew the sky. Besides, when her mom wasn't home, her dad let her eat on the couch, and he never nagged when we wanted to jump on the bed or skip brushing our teeth or play on the roof.

But then her dad died and she grew up and her mother still went on her trips, and Liz had learned to be lonely.

It wasn't the *aloneness* that Liz minded. It was the silence. It *echoed*. It bounced off the walls of the Emerson's oversized house. It filled the corners and the closets and the shadows. In reality, Liz's mom wasn't gone as often as it seemed to Liz, but the silence magnified everything.

It was her oldest fear, that silence. She had always hated

when there was nothing to say, hated the minutes of darkness at sleepovers as everyone drifted but didn't quite sleep, hated study hall, hated pauses in phone calls. Other little girls feared the dark, and they grew up and left their fears behind. Liz was afraid of silence, and she kept her fears clenched so tightly in her fists that they grew and grew and swallowed her whole.

For a while, she sat in the garage with the Mercedes still purring beneath her, the radio blasting line after line of rap she could barely understand. She wished that she'd asked Julia or Kennie to come over after school so she could put off the silence for a little longer. But she hadn't, and she told herself that regret was stupid and she pulled her keys from the ignition. The silence hit her physically, surrounded her as she unlocked the back door, swallowed her as she went inside, strangled her as she slid out of her shoes and microwaved something called a Pizzarito ("a melting pot of flavor!"). Briefly, she thought about going for a run—open gym for soccer would start soon, and she was out of shape—but though the air was crisp and part of her wanted that escape through movement, a greater part was unwilling to go upstairs for her running shoes, come all the way back down, lace them up, dig her keys back out of her purse, lock the door. . . .

The microwave beeped, and Liz fetched the Pizzarito

and flipped through channels until the boredom became intolerable.

Then, with the silence still pounding inside and outside of her, Liz went to the bathroom, slid her fingers down her throat, and carefully transferred the melting pot of flavor from her stomach to the toilet.

In her life, Liz had flirted with a number of dangerous things—drugs, bulimia, the pervert stoner who worked at RadioShack. Bulimia was the only one that stuck. She had broken the habit for a while—she'd started puking blood for a bit, which frightened her, because she hadn't wanted to die. Not then. But she was going to be grinding in a swimsuit tonight, and she wanted to be happy. She wanted to be bright and laughing and thin.

She flushed the Pizzarito and brushed her teeth, but the taste was still there, so she went down to the basement and dug through her mother's enormous wine cabinet and swiped a skinny bottle of—actually, she wasn't really sure what it was, because the words weren't in English, but it was alcoholic and smelled like berries, and the label was pretty—and uncorked it on her way back upstairs. She drank it in bursts, quick head-thrown-back shots, as she went to her room and opened her closet to consider her collection of swimsuits.

The yellow, frilly bikini made her look like a daffodil in

the worst way, the red one was a bit too slutty even for her, and the white bottoms had faded and stretched so much that they now vaguely resembled granny panties. Liz finally settled on the striped maroonish one she'd found on sale at Victoria's Secret a few months before, and she was scrutinizing her hips in the mirror when she caught sight of her fat, bald, hairy, generally pedophilic neighbor standing on his lawn in his bathrobe, squinting at her window.

Liz flipped him off and went back down the hall.

Sometimes, she thought, *this house really is depressing.* But tonight was not going to be one of those nights. It might have started out as one, but the—wine? She thought it was some sort of wine—was taking care of that nicely.

She went back to the living room and turned all of the couch cushions over before she flopped down. The wine sloshed and spilled, and new lavender stains splattered across the older splotches. Once upon a time, she had worried that her mother would discover the mess. She knew better now. Monica was not the type to relax on her overpriced couch. Liz wished she were—she wished that her mother would dig for the remote just once and find the bottoms of the cushions splotched with alcohol, because Liz didn't know how she would react. If she would be angry, if she would finally install a lock on the wine cabinet. If she would care.

Doesn't matter, she thought as she tilted the bottle sharply. *Doesn't matter.*

The liquid spilled over her chin and down her neck and shoulders, and she thought suddenly of the first party she ever went to, the summer before freshman year, and all that had changed since then. She'd had her first beer that night, and her second, her third. She had gotten drunk for the first time, so there wasn't much that she still remembered, not much that she wanted to remember.

She thought of the lights, the bodies, the heavy and shattering music. The air, hot with sweat, humid with guilt.

Doesn't matter.

By eight, half the wine was gone. She could feel the alcohol in her blood, making the world oddly delicate, as though everything had turned brittle and was on the verge of falling apart, and Liz Emerson was the only substantial thing on the planet.

And it was nice, being invincible.

"My god," Julia said as she slid into the passenger seat. "Are you drunk already?"

"Of course," Liz said. She caught a corner of the mailbox as she backed wildly out of Julia's driveway. Later she would find the scratch on the Mercedes, but she didn't care right now. There was something romantic about the idea of being young and tipsy and having somewhere to go on a Friday night.

She handed the berry alcohol stuff to Julia. Julia unstopped the bottle and tilted it back, and though Liz knew that Julia kept her lips tightly closed, she said nothing. It was easier to ignore it. Liz had her occasional trips to the bathroom after dinner, Julia had ziplock bags of illegal substances hidden around her room, and they had an unspoken contract to act as though their own secrets were still, in fact, secret.

"Kennie's riding with Kyle, so you don't need to pick her up," said Julia, handing the bottle back.

Liz snorted. The car swerved as she took a swig, and she laughed as Julia yelped. "She's riding on Kyle, you mean."

"That too." Julia paused for a moment to tighten her seatbelt and then said, quieter, "I can't believe she didn't break up with him."

Liz said nothing. Kennie, of course, was covered by the contract too, and this fell under the list of things Liz didn't want to talk about, things she especially didn't want to talk about tonight.

Stupid, she thought. Four words, four for Kyle to convince her: *But I love you.* And of course they worked, because Kennie would do anything for love.

Stupid, stupid Kennie.

But now Julia was quiet too, remembering that when

it came to staying with cheating boyfriends, Liz had very little to preach about.

Liz pressed down on the gas pedal, then took a hairpin turn that threw a screaming Julia into the door, because tonight, they were unbreakable.

They arrived at the party nearly an hour late, and by then the bonfire was huge and the crowd could be heard from ten blocks away. People were already leaving, because a party of this size, with this much beer, would surely draw as many police officers as a donut buffet. Tyler Rainier was an idiot to throw such a party on a public beach, but Liz didn't care. She took another swig as she got out of the car to make sure she didn't.

Smoke was everywhere, a haze of bonfire and marijuana. There were strobe lights and colored spotlights, and it seemed as though the sky had descended and turned them all to hazy stars. The music made Liz's brain tremble. It was only a matter of time before everyone scattered, but it didn't matter. Not tonight.

Liz glanced at Julia, who was observing the entire thing with an expression that could almost be called disdainful. People called Julia stuck-up because she was quiet and rich and chic and had the posture of a ballerina and was something of a killjoy at parties. Julia was destined for a world of charity balls and pearls. She was a little too smart, a little too graceful, a little too conscientious for this hammered crowd.

And sometimes it made Liz jealous, but tonight was not one of those nights. Tonight, she looked over at Julia and had to fight down the urge to hug her, because Julia was uncomfortable and beautiful and hers.

"C'mon, killjoy," Liz said cheerfully. Julia followed after a moment, and the lights swallowed them together.

"Liz!" Liz almost fell over as Kennie bowled into her. The bottle flew out of her hand and spilled all over Julia.

"Dammit." Julia sighed, looking down at her soaked cover-up. Kennie giggled and licked a drop off her shoulder, ducking away as Julia slapped at her head.

"Get off, lesbo," said Julia, but she was laughing too.

"It's good," Kennie said, picking up the bottle off the sand. She squinted at it. "Oh, my god. I'm not that drunk already, am I? Why can't I read this?"

"Because it's not in English, stupid," said Liz, and Kennie laughed and threw back the rest of the wine. Her hair tumbled down her back, then fanned away as she tossed the bottle at Liz.

"Come on!" Kennie said, grabbing their hands and dragging them into the smoke. The heat was unbelievable; it made Liz's throat itch, and she lifted the bottle again, but it was empty. She dropped it into the sand.

"Careful," she shouted to Julia over the noise. "Don't get too close to the fire! That much alcohol on you—"

"Bitch," Julia called back, shrugging off her soaked clothes. "God, I smell like—"

"Like a Russian!" Liz hollered. She slung an arm around Julia. "Like you're sexy!" She didn't know exactly what she was saying anymore, but who cared? She didn't. She also didn't care about whatever Kennie was babbling about— either Kellie Jensen's outrageous flab or Kyle Jordan's outrageous abs—or about the s'mores and beer that she was trying to pull them toward, so Liz broke away and let the crowd surround her.

Jake Derrick, Liz's official on-again-off-again, was out of state for the weekend at some football camp, most likely hooking up with whichever cheerleader had the biggest boobs, but so what? She grabbed the nearest boy by the belt and he took her hips. It was too smoky and he was too tall for her to make out much of his face, and she didn't try very hard to get a good look. She wasn't here to make memories. She was here for the flashing lights and the sweat and the smoke and the feel of someone else's skin against hers. They were interchangeable, these boys. They didn't matter. They didn't matter at all.

While she was with Boy Number Four, Liz's phone vibrated in her pocket. She pulled it out to see a text from

Julia, saying that she and Jem Hayden, her potentially gay boyfriend, were leaving to check out some indie bookstore. She hadn't seen Kennie for a while, but no doubt she was grinding with Kyle somewhere in the mob.

Doesn't matter. There was too much marijuana in the air, and it was making Liz dizzy. Nothing mattered, not even the way Boy Number Four kept trying to kiss her. Why should it matter? Tomorrow she would wake up and this party would be a haze of lights. She wouldn't remember any of it. So she finally turned her face and let Boy Number Four press his pot-flavored lips to hers, and he wasn't bad.

They hadn't been on the beach for long—half an hour, maybe, and Liz knew this because she had grinded with seven boys so far, one for each song—when they heard the sirens over the music, and then, of course, it was over. As the crowd scattered and someone desperately tried to bury the last keg in the sand, Liz ran. Secretly, she loved when parties were busted. The night wasn't complete without a climax. The sirens, the swirl of red and blue lights—now that was a climax.

So, with a rush of adrenaline, Liz ran, slipping in and out of the crowd. Maybe, in a distant part of her mind, she remembered the games we played together when we were little, pretending to be spies and heroes, always escaping, always invincible.

She jumped into her car and shoved the keys into the

ignition, and backed out of the sand so quickly that she nearly flattened a police officer. She heard him shouting for her to stop, but she didn't listen, and he didn't chase her. Her heart was racing and she was laughing, and she rolled down the windows as she zoomed away so that the night could rush into her car and surround her.

Liz briefly considered going home, but she missed the turn and it was too late to swerve, so she kept going. She pressed down on the gas and soon found herself on the interstate, taking an exit to a place she hadn't been in a decade. She drove along the beach until the trees grew taller and the night grew darker, and she turned in to the entrance of the state park. She parked messily by the ranger station, right next to the sign that said PARK CLOSED. VIOLATORS WILL BE PROSECUTED.

She laughed to herself, thinking of seventh grade, when she, Kennie, and Julia had taken over a janitor's closet and claimed it for themselves. They had made signs like that, VIOLATORS WILL BE PROSECUTED. Or at least, she and Julia had. Kennie's had read PROSECUTORS WILL BE VIOLATED. After thoroughly teasing her for the mistake, they had made that their new motto.

Liz turned off the car and was surprised by the silence. It always surprised her, somehow. She grabbed her iPod and turned it on, breaking the night wide open with shouting and drums, something angry—and then she changed the song, because she was alone, and she didn't have to listen to what other people liked when she was alone.

She forgot, sometimes, that she could make her own choices.

Liz walked into the trees, knowing that she was probably being an idiot and she should at least turn on her flashlight app, but not caring, not caring about anything at all. She hadn't been here since they moved, but her feet still seemed to know the way. She wasn't entirely sure why she'd come at all, now that she thought about it, but that didn't stop her. Liz was beginning to realize that she was drunker than she wanted to admit—enough to be wobbly and careless, and content with being stupid.

She walked in time to some indie singer, who called her beautiful and stronger, stronger, stronger. Liz liked hearing it. She tried to remember the last time she'd heard something like that in real life, and she couldn't. People didn't talk like that anymore, did they?

Liz walked for so long that she was almost entirely certain that she had taken a wrong turn somewhere in the dark, that a bear would be along momentarily to maul her to pieces, eat her left hand, and leave her to bleed to death on the grass just off the trail where no one would find her until she was nothing but a skeleton, which they would ultimately hang up in the science room so that the human anatomy and physiology classes could study her—when, suddenly the trees ended and she saw the tower.

It wasn't as tall as she remembered.

When she was younger, her father would bring her here on the first Wednesday of each month. Her father didn't work on Wednesdays and she didn't have preschool on Wednesdays. Wednesdays were important to them, Wednesdays were *theirs*. They came to make wishes on whatever was around—dandelions in the summer, red and falling leaves in autumn, snowflakes in the winter, sunshine in the spring. Sure, she had been a short four-year-old, but now, staring up at the tower that had once seemed to reach heaven, she finally began to understand how much had changed.

Still, she climbed it. The stairs were steep and creaking. She didn't run up like she used to, because there was no one to race her.

She was more wobbly than ever by the time she got to the top, but she told herself that it was the adrenaline and the height making her sway. When she threw her head back, she could see the sky bending away from her, and it seemed closer than usual. As though if she tried, she could snag a star on her fingernail, but she didn't move.

It hurt, hurt to hold still, so she leaned against the railing with the metal pushing against her lungs, and she closed her eyes.

"Well, hello, darling with the ocean eyes,

How many secrets keep us apart?
A sea of poems, a field of sighs,
Can I cross and return to the start?"

Liz turned off the music. Breathed, and looked up again to face the silence, but it wasn't there. Not the kind she was running from. It was quiet, deeply so, but it was the kind of quiet that lived and moved and *changed*, filled to the brim with crickets and wings and the sounds of late summer.

Later, she lay on her back, staring at the curving sky and the stars, swallowed by the darkness so that she felt very small indeed. She wondered what was between the stars, if it was dead and empty space, or something else. *That's why there are so many constellations,* she thought, remembering the ones from her fourth-grade science class—Leo, Cassiopeia, Orion. Maybe everyone just wanted to connect those pinpricks of brightness and ignore the mysteries in between.

Once upon a time, it made Liz happy to TP a house with Julia and Kennie, to be invited to the best parties. Once upon a time, it made her happy to look down the social tower and see everyone below her. Once upon a time, it made her happy to stand here and see the entire sky above her.

And tonight—tonight, that was what she wished for. She wished to be happy, and fell asleep with an entire sky watching over her.

CHAPTER SIX

If She's Determined

*T*he waiting area of the emergency room is never empty, but right now, it's about as close as it gets. There's a man sitting with his elbows on his knees, staring at the ground. There's a family huddled in a circle, with eyes closed in prayer. There's a boy staring quietly out the window, a name on his lips.

And there, in the far corner, is Liz's mom, quietly eating her last pack of peanuts from the plane and paging through a magazine.

When Liz was younger, people said that she got her face from her mother and everything else from her father. But Liz and her mother share a significant something else that neither of them will ever admit—they both like to play pretend.

So as her daughter lies dying on an operating table, Monica Emerson sits with her legs crossed, looking for all the world like she cares about which celebrity couple broke up this week. On the inside, she shakes to pieces.

She flips a page and thinks of the day Liz learned to walk. Monica had gone to the kitchen to get a box of rice crackers, and when she turned, Liz was standing there behind her, wobbling uncertainly. And even as Monica yelled for her husband to get the camera, she lifted Liz off the ground and back into her arms, thinking *Not yet.*

Not today.

Let her grow up tomorrow.

She flips another page. When she arrived, the doctor told her that even if Liz survives surgery, even if she doesn't die today, *even if,* there's a good chance that she'll never walk again. No one can make promises.

Monica Emerson knows that the likeliest outcome will break her heart, so she does her best not to think about it. She thinks about nothing at all.

That's the thing about Monica Emerson. She is a good person and a terrible mother.

In the operating room, there are tense whispers, the brush of metal against bone, the tinny, faraway beeping that means she's still alive.

And finally, when it's over, the beeping is still there. The doctors are masks and blood splatters, and all I can think is, *This is no miracle.*

One of them—Henderson, according to the blue scribble stitched into his front pocket—breaks away and walks slowly toward the waiting area, which is never a good sign. Doctors with good news are almost as eager to deliver it as the people in the waiting room are to hear it. Only doctors with bad news walk slowly.

Monica rises to meet him, and no one sees how her hands shake as she closes the magazine, lays it down gingerly as though afraid that her trembling will start an earthquake, make the entire world crumble.

But the doctor still walks slowly, and his steps undo her world anyway.

"She isn't looking good," Dr. Henderson tells Liz's mom. For the third time—I've counted. *She isn't looking good, she isn't looking good, she isn't looking good.* "We'll keep a close eye on her for the first twenty-four hours, and reevaluate tomorrow."

But he doesn't really mean it, because he thinks she'll be dead by tomorrow.

As though Monica Emerson could forget, drowning as she is in the list of Liz's injuries. "Her left femur is shattered, and she has a complex fracture in her right hand. She's suffering from massive internal injuries. We've removed her spleen and set the fractures, but her body is still on the verge of shutting down. We're doing everything we can, but at this point, it's up to her."

"What do you mean?"

I am simultaneously resentful of and impressed by Monica's composure. She's so like Liz.

"Liz is strong," the doctor says, as though he has any idea. "She's young, and very fit. She's able to pull through this. If she's determined to, she will."

He goes on to say that their first priority is to stabilize all the hemorrhaging and internal injuries, and they'll do another operation in a few days, *if.* Neither of them notices the boy by the window. He is braced against the arm of his chair and straining to hear. He catches only the worst snatches, "extensive internal bleeding" and "a ruptured lung" and "no one knows" and "but" and "if." The rest is drowned out by the sound of his heart throwing itself against his rib cage.

His name is Liam Oliver. He saw the crumpled, smoking Mercedes at the bottom of a hill on his way to Costco and called the police. Now he sits at the edge of the waiting room, his eyes on the window, her name still on his lips.

He is very much in love with Liz Emerson, and it seems that she will never know.

CHAPTER SEVEN

Pop Quiz

*T*here's something about Julia that makes heads turn.

Even in the emergency room. Even in sweatpants and a shirt that has a hole in the armpit. Even with her smeared eyeliner darkening the circles under her eyes. Even with the scene of the crash still impressed on the insides of her eyelids, so that she sees it every time she blinks.

Even now.

Don't blink, she tells herself as she almost knocks over a table on her way to the nurse's station. She doesn't notice anything, not Dr. Henderson and Monica turning the corner for the ICU, not the classmate sitting by the window.

She had stared at it for so long. There had been so much

traffic. Long, long lines of it, stretching past what remained of Liz's car.

"Hello," says Julia. Hesitantly—Julia is a hesitant person. She turns heads, but she hates being stared at. Once upon a time, she didn't care. But that was a long time ago. "I . . . um. My friend Liz is . . . she was admitted earlier today, I think. Elizabeth Emerson?"

The nurse looks up. "Are you a family member?" she asks.

"No," says Julia, and though she knows the battle is already lost, she can't help but add, "She's my best friend."

It didn't start out that way.

Halfway through seventh grade, Julia's parents decided that they'd had enough of each other. Her mother got the house, all the furniture, a million dollars from her worthless cheating bastard of a husband with sinfully overpriced daughter-stealing lawyers, and her dad, of course, got Julia.

Seventh grade was a horrible year. Seventh grade was puberty. Seventh grade was when Life Learning Skills became about sex and drugs instead of exercise and nutrition. Seventh grade was a year of discovery, of self and survival, of *becoming*. Liz discovered bitchiness, decided selfishness was essential to survival, and became the person she would come to hate. But that was okay, because everyone else acted the same way.

Except Julia.

Julia was . . . different.

Julia didn't wear Crocs. She didn't wear the flowy capri things that everyone else did, she didn't wear her skirts over jeans, she didn't use sports wrap as headbands, she didn't layer her tank tops. She didn't even check her phone all that often. Julia wore brands that the rest of them wouldn't even hear of for another five years. She didn't watch the shows that everyone else watched and she didn't listen to the music the rest of them listened to.

She was brave, and no one is allowed to be brave in middle school.

Liz hated her. She hated her because Julia didn't need to dye her hair or wear makeup to be beautiful, because she just *was*. She hated her because Julia didn't care, didn't care what people thought, didn't care when they stared—not back then. She hated her because Julia was different, and that was enough. Liz hated her, so everyone else did too.

Julia was strange. Julia asked for it. Julia brought it upon herself.

The final straw was this: before Julia had gotten pulled into a higher math class, she was the only one in pre-algebra to ever do her homework. When their teacher one day decided, without warning or precedent, to collect their homework, and Julia was the only one who turned it in, he gave them a pop quiz.

And since she didn't know any of the answers, Liz took a piece of notebook paper and passed it around the class so that each person could write down one thing they thought of Julia.

They said things like "You're not even that pretty" and "Go back to where you came from." Some drew pictures and some drew diagrams, arrows linking words like *weird* and *stuck-up* and *annoying*. When the piece of paper made its way back to Liz, she folded it up and slid it across the table to Julia.

Julia's expression hadn't changed when she read it. She didn't cry, not even a little bit, and heads had swiveled and faces had twisted in surprise, confusion, disbelief—but no one was more shocked than Liz. She could barely keep her jaw from dropping through the floor.

Their teacher gave them a ten-minute warning, and everyone snapped back to attention. Except Julia. Julia was done with her pop quiz, so she flipped the notebook paper over and wrote a single word across the back. Then she folded it into a neat square and passed it back to Liz.

It was the first time Liz had ever been called a bitch.

It was then, in pre-algebra, with a blank pop quiz before her, a wrinkled piece of notebook paper in her lap, and an ugly truth staring up at her, that Liz decided that she and Julia would be friends.

So they were.

Of course Julia took the opportunity. Sadness or popularity? It was not a difficult choice. She used Liz, as anyone else would have. For the first few months, they were not friends, but amid the melodrama, they became allies.

But one day, later that year, as Julia, Liz, and Kennie sat together during a mind-numbing assembly about internet safety, Liz leaned over and whispered to Julia that 34.42 percent of all assembly speakers carried fake boobs around in their briefcases, and when Liz pointed out the speaker's briefcase, Julia had laughed so hard that she had snorted. About six teachers whipped around to shush them, but they had already dissolved into the kind of laughter that made them stupid and helpless, carefree. While the three of them were doubled over, stomachs aching and cheeks cramping, Julia looked over and realized that sometime between *then* and *now*, Liz had become her best friend.

And then she had laughed again, because there was something entirely wonderful about being best friends with Liz Emerson.

CHAPTER EIGHT
Not Yet

*M*onica Emerson loses her composure slowly as she walks toward the ICU. It flakes off and leaves a trail behind her, and I keep my eyes on her face. She's still calm through the first hallway, the second, the third. But as they turn deeper into the hospital, she begins to crack.

She has not cried in public since her husband's funeral. Now she does, knowing that she may soon have to plan her daughter's.

They are small tears, silent, at first—then the doctor opens the doors to the ICU and she sees the rows and rows of beds and bodies, these barely human *things* stuffed full of oxygen and tubes and *not yets*.

She sees Liz among them.

Monica thinks of the maternity ward upstairs, and the tears come a little harder. How Liz had screamed—indignantly, as though they had kept her waiting for too long. She remembers her first moments of motherhood. She does not know how to prepare for her last.

She walks closer and sees Liz beneath a thin blanket, her shoulders wrapped in some hideous hospital thing. Her toes peek out. The nail polish is chipped. Blue, once. Glittery, maybe.

As Monica sits down and looks at the unnatural color of Liz's face, her composure crumbles entirely. There is a very good chance that Liz will die here, two floors beneath where she was born. She will never go to prom, never take her SATs, never apply for college, never graduate, and it's terrifying because Liz already looks dead. Liz looks like she could be packed in a coffin and shoved into the ground.

All Monica wants to do is put her arms around what remains of her daughter, as she hasn't done in so long. But Liz is a tangle of needles and tubes, fragile as ice on an ocean.

So her mother only sits there.

The problem with Monica's brief and imminently ending motherhood is that it was always her greatest fear, being a parent. She doesn't know how to do it, especially not after she buried Liz's father. She had been smothered as a child and she tried too hard to be perfect, and here lies the final proof of her failure.

I almost put my hands on her shoulders—they're thin, sharp, just like Liz's—and tell her *It's okay, it's not your fault, she was already breaking,* but I don't.

It's hard to lie when the truth is dying in front of you.

Monica runs her fingers across Liz's raggedly chewed nails, and she still doesn't see. I forget the lies and try to whisper the truth in her ear, but she can't hear me over the beeping machines.

A nurse watches us. She gives us ten minutes, fifteen, before she breaks away from the clump of monitors in the center of the room. Her scrubs are covered in pink dinosaurs, and they look out of place among the grays and blues—*she* looks out of place, a little too hopeful, a little too brave.

She is very gentle when she touches Monica's arm and says, "I'm sorry. I can't let you stay any longer, ma'am. The risk of infection is too high."

It's kind and very blunt, and I like that she doesn't hide behind bullshit. She doesn't say Liz is strong, because she isn't right now.

Monica almost refuses. But she takes a long look at the stranger who is her daughter, and after a moment, she nods. She reaches out for her, but at the last instant, her fingers tremble and she pulls back.

SNAPSHOT: BAND-AID

Liz is sitting on the kitchen counter, a Band-Aid on her knee. Monica is trying to hug her, and Liz is pushing her away.

A little while before, she had been jumping rope by herself in the driveway, humming the theme song from Arthur. *The world had started coming into focus by then, the sky had grown flat and distant, and I was starting to fade.*

She had jumped three hundred and sixty-eight times when a bug flew into her mouth. She screeched and tripped, her legs tangling in the rope. She fell and tore her knee open, and when I tried to help her, she didn't notice.

She had gone inside, trying very hard not to cry. Monica sat her on the kitchen counter and patched her up, all the while telling her how brave she was. It went to Liz's head a bit, so when Monica tried to hug her, Liz pushed her away and said, "I'm fine, Mom! It's nothing. Just leave me alone."

Monica's heart broke a little bit, and she never tried to hug Liz again.

Later, I would try to push them back together, but neither would budge.

There were little gestures after that—a pat on the back on Christmas, a squeeze across the shoulders on the first day of school. But Monica was too afraid of being overbearing, and Liz tried too hard to be strong.

So there were no more hugs in the Emerson household.

CHAPTER NINE

Voicemail

Monica doesn't go back to the waiting room. She finds a chair and drags it to the hallway outside the ICU, and her arms are shaking so badly that she drops it twice. She positions it beside the doors, reaches into her purse, and pulls out her phone.

She makes three calls. The first, to her boss, to let him know that her daughter is in the hospital and she will not be going to work, or to Bangkok that weekend. The second, to the airline, to cancel her reservation.

And the third, to her daughter, so she can hear her voice on the recorded message.

"Hey. It's Liz. I obviously can't answer at the moment, so leave a message."

Monica calls again and again, and she doesn't know why, but each time she expects a different ending.

CHAPTER TEN

Popularity: An Analysis

*K*ennie half trips off the bus, stretching her sleeping leg as she wobbles across the parking lot. Out of habit, Kennie looks around for Liz's Mercedes, or Julia's Ford Falcon (which, despite Liz's endless teasing and the fact that Julia has access to both of her father's Porsches, she refuses to get rid of). They always went to each other's meets, games, and competitions—she had even sat through their soccer tournaments, every single one, though she never knew when to cheer. But then she remembers that Julia is buried alive in homework and Liz apparently had something else to do today, so no one is here to watch her dance.

That's the thing about Kennie—she has always liked being watched. Whereas Julia dislikes attention and Liz hardly seems to notice it, Kennie needs it like certain other people need cocaine. She's the kind of person who says things that make jaws drop. She likes it when people stare and talk and judge, because it means that someone is always thinking about her. It's what popularity means to her, and Kennie, frankly, has always been popular.

Meridian is a Small Town, the kind that's as faithful to football as religion, the kind with a number of strange habits that define *us* and *them*, the kind with an unspoken and unyielding caste system. Popularity in Meridian extends beyond high school—it encompasses the entire community, the churches and stores and workplaces. There's a clique of ten or so families that has been around for as long as Meridian, and they have spawned nearly all of the jocks, preps, and prom court members. A much greater percentage of the town falls into the social middle: those who live in the small gated community by the country club (because the elite does not, in fact, represent the economic pinnacle of Meridian, and is just the slightest bit resentful of those who do), and almost everyone else. And then there are the shamefully poor, the newcomers, the other anomalies; it is generally agreed that this group is not to be associated with.

Liz knew which group she would be in when she moved to Meridian. I wasn't sure it was a good idea, but she was— she was certain that she knew how to be happy.

The dance team takes their places on stage, and Kennie looks around the crowd again for Liz's face, or Julia's, and she gives a small huff when she doesn't see either. *I'm more important than homework.*

She doesn't think about why she expects them, because her family belongs to the first group. Kennie is always surrounded by friends—her mother is a teacher at the elementary school and the high school track coach, her father is a church deacon and works at the bank and sits on the school board, and her great-great-great-great-grandfather's face is framed in the municipal building alongside the other nine original residents of Meridian.

Liz, a relative newcomer, should have fallen into the last group. For that matter, Julia should have too—and she had, until Liz pulled her out. Kennie doesn't pay attention to popularity much, because she's always had it, but she's suddenly very glad that Liz and Julia fell into the right group, *hers*, even if she doesn't quite know why.

She can't afford to think about it too hard, because the position she holds is an extraordinarily uncomfortable one and the music is about to start. Anyway, Liz is *Liz*. Popularity, Kennie decides, has a lot to do with confidence.

And to Kennie, Liz has more confidence than the rest of Meridian put together.

Despite the fact that Kennie is one of the few people in the world who has seen Liz cry and lash out in frustration, who has seen the part of Liz Emerson that the rest of her tries so hard to hide, Liz is still invincible to her. Whatever Kennie's life looks like from the outside, there is little stability where she stands. Liz is her constant. Liz keeps her steady when her parents fight and her grades dip and her world wobbles.

Kennie counts down the last beats, and bursts into the rehearsed spins and leaps and toe touches, and she doesn't think anymore.

CHAPTER ELEVEN

The Junior Class

"And where did you say you were headed, son?"

"Costco," says Liam. He faces the cop but watches the door out of the corner of his eye. It opens again, and this time the night carries in Lily Maxime and Andrea Carsten, who are undoubtedly here to confirm the rumors. They hate Liz Emerson because she ignored them. Their eyes are red, and they start sobbing when they reach the group of Meridian students huddled around a low table.

There are a hundred and forty-three students in Liam's graduating class, and a good third of them are here tonight. He can't figure out why. Liz Emerson slipped on the goddamn road—clearly tonight is not a night to be driving around in the dark.

"I was running errands for my mom," he adds.

"And you saw Elizabeth's car as you drove past?"

Liz Emerson, he corrects automatically in his head. She is always Liz Emerson to him. He doesn't think he knows her well enough to call her exclusively by her first name. But then again, he doesn't know her well enough to think of her as often as he does, either.

"Yeah."

"How did you know it was her car?"

"I'd know her car anywhere."

This he says without thinking, and regrets it when the police officer asks, "Were you good friends?"

"No," says Liam. "Not really."

Not at all.

The police officer gives him a strange look. Liam doesn't care. He is watching his classmates again, huddled around each other and whispering, crying into each other's shoulders. Not just crying—sobbing these awful sobs that made everything shake, and Liam wants to scream that she isn't dead. She is alive right now, down the hall somewhere—not whole, but alive, and everyone is sobbing like she's already gone.

Half of these people have no reason to be here. Most

of these people, really. Liam wonders what Liz Emerson would do if she knew that Jessie Klayn, who flips her off once a day when her back is turned, had already gone through an entire box of tissues. And Lena Farr too—Lena Farr, who had spent all of lunch today ranting about what a selfish bitch Liz Emerson is. Liam has heard it all from the next table over.

Laugh, probably. Liz Emerson would laugh, and he is glad she isn't here to see it, because Liz Emerson did not have a nice laugh anymore. She had a laugh like a knife on skin.

"All right," says the police officer. "Well, that's it for now. We might track you down later, though, kid."

"I'll be here."

He doesn't know he means it until he says it aloud.

Liz is not a selfish bitch.

If she were, she wouldn't have planned anything, everything.

But she did.

CHAPTER TWELVE

Three Weeks Before Liz Emerson Crashed Her Car

*I*t was January 1, and Liz had just come home to an empty house after a New Year's Eve party.

She was drunker than she had ever been in her life, and it was not a particularly enjoyable experience. She stumbled into the foyer and leaned against the door to keep herself upright, and swallowed a few times to delay the puke. When she closed her eyes, she could still see the pulsing lights impressed upon her personal darkness, and it made her dizzy. She gave up, and slid to the floor, her head pounding, everything spinning. She needed someone, anyone, to touch her and remind her that she wasn't the last person in the world.

She opened her eyes and found the chandelier instead. The light was blinding, like angels, like angels falling and flying and coming for her, and she tried to think of a reason to go on.

She couldn't.

But she could think of a thousand reasons to give up. She thought of her father dying. She thought of how her mother wouldn't be home for another week. She thought of Kyle Jordan's lips on hers and his hands on her body, just an hour ago. And she closed her eyes, and thought about how he was Kennie's boyfriend, but she had kissed him back anyway, because she had never felt so alone as she had then, drunk and stupid and trying not to cry at a stranger's party.

But, god, how could she explain that to Kennie?

She couldn't, ever. She opened her eyes again. The light still stabbed and the angels still fell, and she began to plan her suicide.

She thought of stuffing herself with pills. She thought of filling her bathtub with water and making those long cuts across her arms. She thought of scarves and pantyhose, and hanging from the loft like an ornament. She thought of a quick shot, a bright explosion. But they didn't have a gun. Did they?

Liz couldn't remember. She couldn't remember anything.

She was curled in a ball in the middle of the foyer when the numbness faded and the tears came, and she sobbed with her face pressed against the hardwood. She washed the floor with her tears and polished it with her snot, and finally she had three rules.

First, it would be an accident. Or it would look like one. It would look like anything but suicide, and no one would ever wonder what they did wrong, what made her give up. She would die, and maybe everyone would forget that she had ever lived.

Second, she would do it in a month. Well, three weeks. She would do it on the tenth anniversary of the day her dad fell off the roof and broke his neck. She would give her mother just this one day of sadness every year, instead of two.

And three, she would do it somewhere far away. She wanted a stranger to find her body, so no one she loved would see her broken.

They didn't work, her rules.

Liam found her. Liam, who had loved her since the first day of fifth grade, was driving down the interstate when he turned and saw her, the bright green of her sweater visible through what remained of the window.

Her mother is crying silent tears in the hallway outside

the ICU, whispering her daughter's name and her husband's name, over and over again like a prayer, the tears pooling on the backs of her shaking hands and falling, falling, falling.

And I won't forget. I promise her what no one else can. I promise her, *always*.

CHAPTER THIRTEEN
Midnight

*I*t's very quiet. Distant buzzing, background beeping. The waiting room is mostly empty. Liam has fallen asleep. The zipper of his hoodie is caught between his face and the window, imprinting the pattern of teeth across his cheek and lips. In his pocket, his dying phone vibrates with yet another call from his frantic mother, but it isn't enough to wake him up.

Down the hall, Monica Emerson is asleep too, her head against the wall. The nurse with the pink dinosaurs on her scrubs walks by and sees her, and goes for a blanket. As she tucks it around Monica's shoulders, Monica stirs and whispers her daughter's name.

△▽△

Upstairs, Julia sits in the cafeteria with her fingers wrapped around her third Red Bull. Tonight is the first time she's ever tried one. She doesn't like the taste, not at all, and she hates the tremors, but at least she's awake. She must stay awake, and she repeats it to herself as though it'll keep her eyelids from fluttering shut. She can't sleep tonight. She won't. She must be awake when—if, *if*—bad news comes, because she cannot bear the idea of waking to it.

Kennie is just getting home. The competition results got delayed due to some scoring mix-up, and they were there for hours longer than they should have been. It doesn't matter. They won.

Cheeks sore, stomach cramped.

She slips through the garage door into a dark house. Her parents are both awake in their separate bedrooms, her father working and her mother reading, but she doesn't want to see either of them. She needs to charge her phone—it is dead in her pocket, and their coach has a strict "no phones at competitions" rule, anyway. They're supposed to focus or bond or some other crap, though no one would have agreed to it had there been any service at all. She plugs it in and goes to the bathroom.

Shower. Sparkles and spandex for a worn pair of pajamas.

She comes back and checks her phone in the dark—her mother has just yelled for her to go to bed, she has school tomorrow—and opens her Facebook app.

Wet hair atop her head, a story through statuses.

Oh my god I can't believe it Liz Emerson crashed her car she's in the hospital she doesn't look good she's dying she's dead she's not she is be safe Liz we're praying for you we're praying praying praying.

She screams for her parents and runs into the hallway with the screen of her phone glaring. They refuse to let her drive to the hospital.

She goes back to her room with sobs tearing her apart. She lies in the darkness, surrounded by pillows and an impossible amount of fear.

SNAPSHOT: TWO

We're on the roof. It's flat, a balcony that they never added a railing to. A few feet away, Liz's father is fixing a leak.

She is pulling the chalk across the freezing surface and singing. Her breath hangs in the air. She draws two little girls, as always. The first looks like her—a bundle girl today, boots and hat and puffy cloud coat. The second is never the same.

Today, I wear a pink sequined dress. I have the hair of her favorite doll and a pair of shoes she's designing herself.

The wind invites the powder snow to dance, and the sun is everywhere. Soon, we will get bored and put the chalk away, but right now, we are happy. We draw. We sing.

She finishes the heel of my shoe. Her fingers are chapped.

It is the last picture I will ever be in.

CHAPTER FOURTEEN

Fifty-Eight Minutes Before Liz Emerson
Crashed Her Car

She was still in Meridian then, just turning onto the interstate. Her backpack was beside her in the passenger seat—exams started next Monday, so it held every single one of her textbooks. She had filled it out of habit, and now she wished she hadn't. Textbooks were expensive.

Her grades were still mostly decent, if only because someone was sure to notice if they had nose-dived. She was glad her GPA was still intact. At least something was.

No, she remembered. She hadn't finished the last physics project; her grade, which had been hovering precariously at a C minus, had surely dipped with that zero. She'd managed to keep an A until they started talking about

Newton—whom Mr. Eliezer had introduced as a lifelong virgin, like, *Let's study this dude who was so obsessed with physics that he didn't even want to have sex, isn't he incredible?*—and somewhere in the sudden flood of velocity and inertia and force, Liz had started falling behind.

She just didn't get physics. So there were all these theories and laws, and they'd spend weeks picking them apart, and in the end, Mr. Eliezer would tell them that they had to factor in air resistance and friction and all this other crap, so most of them couldn't even be applied. It seemed sketchy to her, a science dependent upon the uncertainties of life.

Still. It was nice, the idea that she would never have to stress about homework or grades or Newton the goddamn virgin ever again.

But she turned onto the on-ramp too sharply, and her backpack kept moving in one direction while the car turned in another. It thudded to the floor of the car, and Liz starting thinking about moving objects and Newton's First Law.

Objects at rest stay at rest, objects in motion stay in motion.

CHAPTER FIFTEEN

One Day After Liz Emerson Crashed Her Car

*L*iz has always hated missing school. She hates making up work and wondering what happened without her. Did people talk about her? Did they call her slut and skank and worse things while she was gone? She always talks about people behind their backs, so she assumes that everyone else does too. Liz has gone to school with hangovers and migraines, bruises and sprains, colds and stomach flus, and once with a sore throat that started an epidemic of strep throughout the entire district.

But today, with a missing spleen and a broken leg and a shattered hand and a ruptured lung and too much internal bruising to document, it seems unlikely that

Liz Emerson will attend school.

Julia too stays at the hospital with what must be her tenth can of Red Bull wobbling in her hands. Monica is there, of course, and Liam, who hadn't intended to stay at the hospital all night, is still asleep against the window.

Everyone else is already at school. Within the walls of Meridian High School, there is a hush like smoke, like smog. Breathing it is like breathing January air—it stings with each inhale, freezes inside each lung. An hour away, Liz is dying in St. Bartholomew's, but here, she is already dead. The rumors have made it very clear that there is little hope for Liz Emerson.

The worst place is the cafeteria, where most of the school congregates before the bell rings, copying homework and gossiping. I get a glimpse as I walk by, a glimpse of the shock and tears, and it's so strange, the silence, the sniffling.

How Liz would have hated it.

She would have known that most of them aren't crying for her. They're crying for themselves, for fear of death, for the loss of faith in their own invincibility, because if Liz Emerson is mortal, they all are.

The teachers are having an emergency faculty meeting, where they receive hastily photocopied sheets of "Things to Say to Distraught Students." The principal breaks down when she tells everyone that the only reason Liz is still alive is because a machine is moving her lungs.

But I think at least a few of the teachers must be relieved, just a little, that Liz Emerson is no longer going to be attending their classes. Spanish, because Liz blatantly texted every single day and never participated in class. English, because Liz deliberately formed opinions directly opposite those of the teacher's. Definitely study hall, because Liz Emerson's very presence inspired everyone else to do stupid things.

It isn't that Liz minds authority, exactly. It's just that she once liked being Liz Emerson and she liked showing it, and that meant challenging teachers and daring them to challenge her back. And it doesn't matter that she grew to hate it—she couldn't stop.

The teachers who cry: Ms. Hamilton, who teaches psychology and cries at everything; Mrs. Haas, who teaches world history and was actually worried out of her mind; and Mr. Eliezer, Liz's physics teacher.

He scratches his jaw, and no one notices the tears in his eyes. It seems unlikely that Liz will ever get her physics grade back up.

Liz Emerson had failed physics so utterly that she couldn't even crash her car right.

△ ▽ △

Upstairs, Kennie's sobbing fills the hallway—it's louder, perhaps, than strictly necessary. Everyone is watching her, and a small and despicable part of Kennie enjoys the attention. She doesn't bother feeling guilty about it. Her best friend is dying, and her other best friend didn't even call her with the news.

Kennie finds comfort in not being alone; Julia finds it in the quiet. So Julia is still at the hospital, where Monica has finally found her, and Kennie is a mess of running mascara.

Liz, though, found her brand of comfort—numbness, forgetting—in throwing things and watching them shatter. She found it in taking her Mercedes out and driving thirty, forty above the speed limit, with the sunroof open so that the wind whipped her hair all around her. She found it in being reckless, careless, stupid.

Once, Liz found comfort in me. Once, she found it in holding my hand and dreaming until our dreams came true. Once, she found it in simply being alive. Eventually, she could no longer find comfort in anything. By the end, she was just another girl stuffed full of forgotten dreams, until she crashed her car and she wasn't even that.

CHAPTER SIXTEEN

Empty Seat

Liz has photography first hour, and nothing gets done without her. Kennie and Julia are supposed to be in this class too, but they don't make it. The majority of the class—the girls, at least—sits in tears, and Mr. Dempsey, the art teacher, is more than willing to let them take it easy. He is terrified that he might actually have to use the "Things to Say to Distraught Students" handout.

He goes to his office and pulls Liz's portfolio out of his filing cabinet; he flips through her photos, black-and-white prints, colored and edited ones, and tries to remember the girl behind the camera. Most of the shots have hasty Bs dashed across the backs.

Mr. Dempsey is the kind of teacher who gets so caught up with a piece of canvas that he often fails to notice when students walk in and out of class. He ignores bells and schedules, fails to hear fire drills (though, admittedly, that's only happened once so far), and he typically grades haphazardly, at the last minute. It's not that he doesn't care. It's just that he usually forgets.

Liz has never made much of an impression on him. He knows Julia much better, because she's the most talented student he's ever had, and they have had long discussions about aperture and different lighting techniques and the best brand of Earl Grey tea. And he has no choice but to know Kennie, because he's always telling her to shut up or sit down or not to spill that particular caustic chemical. Liz, though—this was perhaps the one class that Liz Emerson sat through quietly. This class appealed to the little girl she wasn't anymore, the part of her that was still amazed every time she clicked the shutter and captured a moment.

And her photos. Mr. Dempsey's vision blurs slightly as he sifts through them. There are close-ups of gravel strewn across a lawn. Tire tracks in the parking lot. Flowers too close to the road. Trampled, frost-choked grass. A cloudy sky through bare branches.

The emotion disarms him. He has never noticed the

rawness of Liz Emerson's photos before, and now he sits guilt-stricken as he realizes that this is the first time he has really looked at them.

The photos slide off his lap and onto the floor. He makes a halfhearted attempt to catch them, but then lets them fall, watching as they drift down around him.

He leans back in his chair and just looks at it all, the final diary of a dying girl.

Second hour pre-calc is filled with jocks and preps and other social elites whom Liz considered more than acquaintances but less than friends. They considered themselves much more than that, though, so when Ms. Greenberg says, "Take out last night's assignment," the class just stares at her.

Finally, a braver and slightly desperate student speaks up. "C'mon, Ms. Greenberg. You can't really think that we're able to concentrate at a time like this. . . ."

Ms. Greenberg fixes him with her piercing signature stare. "Were you at the hospital last night, Mr. Loven?"

"No," he mutters.

"Then I expect you were neither physically nor emotionally incapable of completing your assignment. Should I mark you down as a zero?"

Turns out, most people didn't finish the assignment. Ms.

Greenberg docks points from all of them.

After going over the homework and answering questions for the three people who actually did it, Ms. Greenberg, ignoring the incredulous stares of the class, hands out note packets for the lesson. She writes Liz's name across the top of one and puts it in the folder marked ABSENT.

"Ms. Greenberg . . ."

"Yes?"

Carly Blake hesitates. She plays soccer with Liz and they usually sit at the same lunch table, but she's no closer to Liz than any of her other more-than-acquaintances-less-than-friends, and I think Ms. Greenberg knows this. Certainly her look doesn't waver as Carly's lip wobbles.

"I just don't think . . . I just don't know if we can—I mean, Liz is just so . . . and we're all so worried . . ."

Ms. Greenberg actually glares at her, and Carly trails off into silence. Ms. Greenberg puts down the note packets and looks around the classroom. No one meets her eyes.

"All right," she says. "That's enough. I want you all to remember that Ms. Emerson is not dead. Stop acting like she is. Until I have been notified that she is, indeed, destined for a coffin, I refuse to believe that she is. So yes, I will hold her notes and schedule a day for her to make up her quiz, though I'm sure she'll blatantly ignore both. For those of you who are using Liz's accident as a reason to neglect your work, I assure you it's a weak and despicable excuse."

If another teacher had given such a speech, the class would have mutinied. A lot of things can be said about the student body of Meridian High school, but no one can accuse them of disloyalty. Liz is *theirs*, and they would have defended her to the death—or to a detention, whichever came first—if they needed to.

But Ms. Greenberg has long been loved and hated for her bluntness, and there's something in her gaze that makes them all feel terribly ashamed.

There, in that classroom, I feel the tides turning. The period ends, and everyone rushes off. The rumors shift. All gossip, they say. Liz isn't on her deathbed. Liz is no longer dead, but recovering. After all, she is Liz Emerson.

Just before third period, Julia comes back to school. For the first time in her life, she is a mess.

Having spent the night at the hospital, she wears the same sweatpants and shirt with the hole in the armpit. There are shadows beneath her eyes, and she is so pale that her skin is almost green.

From the moment she steps foot in the building, she is surrounded by sympathizers, but she hardly notices.

Julia has had her share of tragedy over the years, but

they were tragedies contained within her world—her parents' divorce, her brittle and strained relationship with her father, the death of her gerbil. Liz's accident, however, is a terrifyingly immense thing, and try as she might, Julia cannot keep it within herself.

She left the hospital in a vain attempt to escape it. She came to school, and it found her here too.

Next, chemistry.

Liz was supposed to take it during her sophomore year, but due to scheduling conflicts and an extraordinarily unhelpful counselor, she is stuck taking both chemistry and physics during her junior year.

It's really a pity, because Liz had been looking forward to chemistry since the brief unit in sixth grade. It was the colors that had initially attracted her, the vibrant blue of the Bunsen flame and the dusty red of copper and the deep violet of permanganate. It was the logic of balanced equations, the certainty that when element A mixed with element B, compound C would appear. It was like predicting the future; it was like magic. Most of all, it was *being*: of having to be so careful with the hydrochloric acid, of accidentally burning herself while lighting a match, of discovering.

Only, by the time she finally got to take the class, school had already stopped mattering.

Today there is no lab. There is no lecture. The class sits silently, in a darkness lit only by the episode of *MythBusters* on the screen.

They stare at the empty chair. They remember the first day of fifth grade, when Liz arrived and disrupted Meridian as only she could. Liz Emerson, they think, has always been a force to be noticed.

They are wrong.

CHAPTER SEVENTEEN

Before

On the first day of preschool, Liz dug her fingers into the leg of her father's jeans and held on tight as the overly sunny teacher tried to drag her into the overly sunny classroom.

Her dad leaned down and told her to make a wish.

Tearfully, Liz asked her daddy to stay with her.

He promised to never leave.

On the first day of school after her father's funeral, Monica dropped Liz off for the first time. Monica didn't try to hug her, and Liz didn't ask her to stay.

△▽△

On the first day of fifth grade at Meridian Elementary School, Liz jumped off the swings during recess and headed for the kickball diamond. She kicked a ball into Jimmy Travis's face, gave him a bloody nose, won her team the game, and sat down at the popular table during lunch without being asked. She never left.

On the first day of middle school, Liz walked into the building with Kennie at her side. At recess that day, Jimmy Travis told her that she was pretty, and she kissed him beside the swings.

They were the first official couple.

She dumped him two weeks later when he refused to let her copy his math homework, and from then on, Liz Emerson was rarely without a boyfriend.

She didn't really like any of them.

On the day after eighth-grade graduation, she went to her first party and kissed an older boy named Zack Hayes, who he had given her a red Solo cup. She tried the beer and hated it, but she drained the cup anyway and he refilled it for her. It made the world dissolve and scatter around her like petals, and it wasn't unpleasant. When she wobbled and fell, he caught her and carried her into a bedroom but didn't leave, and she couldn't find the words to ask him to.

Julia found them later and pulled her away, but Liz wasn't sure what had happened before she got there.

On the first day of her freshman year, an upperclassman named Lori Andersen elbowed Liz into a locker and called her a stupid freshman.

During lunch, Liz stole Lori's car keys while Lori was in the lunch line, turned the car alarm on, and threw the keys in a toilet. Then, while Lori was fuming, Liz offered her sympathies and a coupon to the salon for a free facial waxing. Lori, who had an unfortunate habit of underestimating freshmen, took it.

That particular salon was owned by Kennie's uncle. He'd opened it when he got out of prison and found out that he could get paid to pull hair out of people.

Liz called him and told him that Lori would be coming by after school. She asked him to please give her the special, free of charge. He replied that it would be his pleasure.

The next day, Lori came to school with newly cut bangs. It wasn't the best look for her, though her friends assured her that it was adorable. It went well until Lori went outside for gym, and the wind blew her bangs back.

It was then that everyone saw that Lori Andersen no longer had eyebrows.

Liz took Lori's place at the Center Table in the Cafeteria

That Looked Exactly Like All the Other Tables but Held Immense Social Meaning.

Later, she would wonder what would have happened if she had let her world change as it should have changed. On nights when she remembered Lori Andersen's missing eyebrows, she told herself that it would have happened anyway. Lori's grades would have dropped anyway. She would have had to work at Subway instead of going to college anyway.

And besides, her eyebrows grew back.

CHAPTER EIGHTEEN
Ziplock Bags

*L*iz's next class is government. They were supposed to debate the death penalty, but today, even the affirmative squad wants to argue that no one deserves to die.

Besides, they're missing a member of their team.

Liz is not fantastic at debate, pointwise. She just happens to like arguing, and she has an incredible talent for making others look stupid.

Julia is also in this class, but she hates debating. It isn't that she's not eloquent—she could probably win every debate based on her vocabulary alone—but she doesn't understand absolutes. She doesn't see why one side is completely right and the other completely wrong.

Which isn't to say that Julia is any more secure in her morals than Liz is. Julia has plenty of issues, the greatest being the ziplock bag she buys from the RadioShack pervert every Sunday after church.

Julia sits there and thinks about the fight she and Liz had the day before yesterday. Just two days ago. Julia glances at the clock and hates it for its blind, relentless ticking, because every moment that passes is another step from yesterday, when Liz was whole and alive, and the world was all right.

It was an old fight. Or at least it had brewed for long enough—two days ago it had simply exploded, burst from both of them, and now it stretches across the hours and hours to hang over them like a storm.

Julia wants to go back to the hospital. She wants to apologize. No, she wants to say that she will do as Liz asked, she will get help, she will move the world to keep Liz Emerson alive.

But she can't. Get help, or move the world.

Instead she thinks about how it all began, and the regret grows and grows until it's almost a tangible thing that she can rip out and bury and undo.

Almost.

△ ▽ △

It started after their freshman homecoming game. They were sitting behind the bleachers with an innocuous bag of white powder, which Liz had seen peeking out of a stranger's pocket. Naturally, she had stolen it so they could try it. Just a little bit each. Kennie was excited, because she was Kennie and new things, no matter how stupid, made her bounce. Liz was rather indifferent to it all. She was only doing it because she was Liz Emerson.

But Julia—Julia was skeptical on the outside and so, so scared on the inside. Her hands were shaking as she watched Liz inhale, as Kennie tried and choked and got it in her eyes. Her hands shook as she took the bag and opened it, and they shook when she hesitated.

Liz laughed.

Julia did it because of the way Liz stared at her, daring her to take the risk for once. So she did. She took the risk while Liz and Kennie forgot everything their middle-school health teacher had ever taught them—assuming that they had actually listened in the first place. That drugs worked differently on everyone. That you really could get addicted on the first try.

Julia remembered. It didn't matter.

Soon Kennie couldn't sit still, Liz was laughing, and Julia was still shaking. Pleasantly, at first, but as the other two began to quiet down, she shook harder because her fingers kept reaching for more, until there was none left.

Two days before Liz crashed her car, Julia decided that she'd had enough. Her grades were slipping, and sometimes she couldn't breathe. Her father had just lost some money on the stock market and was still paying ridiculous amounts of alimony, and her "borrowed" drug allowance wouldn't go unnoticed for much longer.

And Liz—well, Liz was fine, wasn't she? She wasn't throwing money at the RadioShack guy. She didn't know about Julia's Sundays, when the world was so bright it hurt her eyes, but she was in the dark, alone, trapped in a body that would never again obey her mind.

I didn't ruin my life, Liz. You did.

But now Liz is almost gone and Julia sits choking on regret, and that's the ironic thing—why didn't she feel guilty earlier? Why only now, now that Liz is dying in a white room beneath fluorescent lights? Why is it that she's remembering the way Liz's face looked after Julia had thrown the blame at her?

She'd had thestrangest expression. Like something was breaking inside of her too.

Julia stares at the clock. She imagines climbing on the

desk and pulling it down, rewinding the hands and praying the rest of the world would follow. She sees the bodies blurring and walking backward, until she is in the hallway again with Liz right there, begging her to stop, stop, get help.

She wonders what might have been different if she'd agreed.

The bell rings, and Julia walks out of the classroom and out the door. The one by the band room, the one no one ever watched, the one in a nook away from the cameras. She, Liz, and Kennie had done it a hundred times before.

She heads back to the hospital.

Funny things, aren't they? People. They're so limited.

Seeing is believing and all that. As though watching Liz will keep her alive. As though by remembering, they know her, intimately. As though they guard all of her secrets, and by staying close, they can keep her safe.

I think it must be because they can only see so much of the world. All those boundaries—pupils to focus, lids to close, distances to cross, time to navigate.

Don't they realize?

Thought exists everywhere.

What Julia doesn't know is this: Liz knew. Liz had always known that the drug was tearing Julia's life apart.

She knew that it was her fault. She knew that the ziplock bags made Julia lonely, but she didn't know how to help.

Some nights, Liz looked back and counted the bodies, all those lives she had ruined simply by existing. So she chose to stop existing.

CHAPTER NINETEEN

The Brown Couch, New Year's Day

After Liz puked, she went down to the basement with a marker and sat on the couch.

The couch—an old brown thing, stained with memories and orange juice instead of hangovers and wine. Monica had stored it down here after she bought the white couch, and when Liz put her face in the fabric, it smelled of dust. No one came down here much. This couch was one of the last pieces of furniture from their old house, from that other life, when Liz had a father who would never leave and a mother who didn't have any grief to bury in her work.

When she had me.

She rolled up her sleeve and wrote her three rules across her arm, so she wouldn't forget. She underlined them, and added:

HERE LIES LIZ EMERSON.

SNAPSHOT: HIDING

The house is white with blue shutters, and there is something indefinably cozy about it. To the side, Liz is behind a bush, her hands pushing the leaves apart. We have played at least a thousand games of hide-and-seek here. Liz counts to a hundred and then searches everywhere, as though she can't hear me giggling, as though I ever hide anywhere except behind the brown couch.

Soon Liz will begin to grow up. The older she gets, the less interested she will be in searching, the more easily distracted she will be by television and snacks and stories, the less she will care if I am ever found.

One day, she will count, and I will hide behind the brown couch.

She will forget to seek.

CHAPTER TWENTY

Fifty-Five Minutes Before Liz Emerson Crashed Her Car

She was sharply aware of the time slipping through her fingers, and she wondered if it had always passed this quickly. Yesterday she was getting her first bra, and the day before that she was graduating from elementary school. A week ago, she had taken the training wheels off her bike all by herself and had ridden almost five feet before the entire bike fell apart because she had loosened one screw too many.

If only time had moved as quickly during physics class.

Outside the car, it had started snowing again. Little specks like dandruff. *Gravity,* thought Liz. *Goddamn gravity,* and all of a sudden those suppressed twinges of sadness flared into something much greater. She would never understand, would she? Gravity and inertia, force and mass and acceleration—she would never know *why*.

She glanced at her clock and thought, *I still have time. Objects at rest.*

But it was like taking a timed test, and her mind did what it always did during timed tests. It wandered, and soon Liz was thinking about fourth grade, the year before her mother was promoted and they moved to Meridian. They were all objects at rest, then.

Fourth grade was fuzzy—she remembered only the most vague and cliché of events—playing kickball at recess, cutting in the lunch line, getting caught and subsequently sentenced to five minutes on the Wall. Fractions.

Liz had no real friends back then. There were people with whom she was friendly, she sat in a big group at lunch, and she had a reasonable amount of fun. But her friends were interchangeable. Somehow, they all felt temporary.

And she certainly hadn't belonged to the group of girls who wore matching skirts and sneakers from Target. *That* Liz Emerson had been content in her place just outside the spotlight. She was comfortable with her quiet half anonymity.

There was one girl in particular, Mackenzie Bates, who was enormously popular by fourth-grade standards, which mostly meant that she brought the best lunches in the prettiest lunch boxes and was the tallest girl in the class. When Mackenzie spoke, the fourth grade listened.

A few months into the year, a girl named Melody Lace Blair arrived at school. Her parents were hippies from California, and Melody came to class in overalls—*overalls*, the deadliest and ugliest sin. That would have been enough reason to exclude her even if Mackenzie hadn't developed an immediate and intense hatred for her.

Not only did they share initials, but Melody was exactly one inch taller than Mackenzie.

It had started small. Snide whispered comments. Glares from the opposite side of the room. But soon Mackenzie got her group of matching friends in on it, and things began to escalate.

At one point or another, most of the fourth graders remembered all of the antibullying assemblies they had sat through. They recalled how eagerly they had agreed to speak up if they saw someone being bullied.

But slowly, then with more force, the fourth grade came to agree with Mackenzie. Melody was different, different was weird, weird was bad. It was simple. Maybe they didn't actively participate in the undoing of Melody Blair, but it was their silence, their willingness to look away, that lent Mackenzie her power.

So as everyone else became blind in matters concerning

Melody, Liz kept watching. She tried to understand why everyone was so afraid of being different—why she was too. A hundred times she opened her mouth to speak up for Melody, and a hundred times she closed it. It would have been a one-way ticket to the center of the shooting range.

Say something, I told her, and told her again. *Say something. You promised.*

She wasn't listening.

The final showdown happened in early spring, one of the first days after they were allowed outside for recess again. Maybe Mackenzie was bored, or maybe the change in the weather also called for a change in playground patterns, or maybe she was just experiencing early puberty—whatever the reason, she cornered Melody and tore her apart with words.

It didn't take long for the rest of the fourth graders to notice and migrate over. Liz had been on the monkey bars with some other girls, but one by one, they left to watch. Finally, Liz did too. She couldn't help it. There was a certain dark allure in destruction, and who was Liz to defy it?

Standing as part of the silent majority, Liz was not the only one who felt guilty. Guilt, however, wasn't enough of a force to push them from the winning side. So Liz and everyone else stood and listened as Mackenzie and her friends grew more and more vicious.

"You're so ugly that you probably break every mirror you pass."

"Your clothes are, like, totally hideous."

"You smell so weird. Take a shower, loser."

Amid the hoots and jeers of his group of miniature-jock friends, Mack Jennings shouted something about Melody being fat, and within minutes, everyone had arranged themselves into a loose ring. One by one, they went around the circle and stated one thing that they disliked about Melody.

When Liz found herself in that circle, she did not move.

I tried to push her, but I didn't have enough force, either.

They were barely a quarter of the way around when Melody began to cry. She stood surrounded, wide-eyed and lost, shaking and afraid and confused and searching for answers in eyes that refused to meet hers.

"Why do you always walk with your nose up in the air like that? Do you think you're better than us or something?"

"Is there something wrong with your feet, or do you always walk like a cripple?"

Then it was Liz's turn. When she hesitated, everyone turned to look at her, and Liz looked at Melody. She looked at the tear-streaked face and the red eyes, and she saw something that made her want to cry too.

"Liz," Mackenzie said impatiently.

Liz opened her mouth and said in a quiet rush, "When's your birthday?"

There was a small, confused silence. In it, Liz saw Melody's hope grow infinitesimally, so Liz looked away when she ripped it to shreds.

"I think I'll buy you a dictionary," she said. Still rushing, the words falling and splattering like rain. "So you can look up 'normal.' You obviously don't know what it means."

Mackenzie laughed. Everybody laughed.

Liz stared at the ground.

I tried to take her hand, but she was slipping away.

Then, suddenly, Melody pushed through the mob and ran into the building. The recess monitors, who were busy trying to wrestle the kindergarteners off the climbing wall, noticed nothing. Mackenzie didn't move for a moment, disoriented now that her circus act had disappeared. Then she blinked a few times and skipped away with her friends. Bit by bit, everyone else broke off too.

Except Liz. She waited until no one was watching, and headed inside.

She checked the classroom and the cubby room, and when she didn't find Melody, she went to the girls' bathroom. Sure enough, she heard the sobs as soon as she pushed open the door. She stepped carefully, her sneakers almost silent against the tiles, and she saw Melody's feet dangling beneath the stall door as she sat and cried.

But in the end, Liz did nothing. She watched for another moment, and then she went back outside and joined her friends by the monkey bars.

Liz would remember that day while sitting in pre-algebra with a blank pop quiz in front of her. Mackenzie was the inspiration for the piece of paper she sent around the class, on which everyone wrote one thing they disliked about the new girl with the weird clothes, and it was partly because of the dangling feet, watching them, that she ultimately befriended Julia.

One day, years later, Liz went to the beach with Kennie and Julia. Kennie was in the water and Julia was asleep in the sun, and Liz was trying to clean the sand off her phone when she saw an obituary for a girl named Melody Lace Blair, who had been found dead in her bathtub. The police suspected suicide.

Liz's old town had held a memorial service, according to the obituary. When the students gathered together to remember Melody, one girl gave a moving speech about the beautiful, strong, wonderful person Melody had been, and how she would never be forgotten.

Funnily enough, the speaker had the exact same initials as Melody.

CHAPTER TWENTY-ONE

Fifty Minutes Before Liz Emerson Crashed Her Car

She gripped the steering wheel and wondered if Melody had known.

That Liz had been there.

That she had watched her feet dangle.

She couldn't have. If she had, she would have said something. After all, they had been alone. Melody could have insulted Liz all she liked—she would have, if she had known Liz was there, surely she would have. She could have said the most awful thing in the world, and Liz wished that she had. Because then she could die believing that humans were inherently crappy creatures, and maybe her conscience would be a little lighter on this particular drive.

But part of Liz wondered if Melody had already learned what it had taken Liz sixteen years to figure out (and even then, only by ripping off the Gandhi quote she'd come across in her history textbook): that taking an eye for an eye left the whole world blind.

Objects at rest. Standing and watching, watching and standing.

How do you gather the force to push an object into motion?

Was it a riddle? A test question? It didn't matter. She knew the answer.

She drove faster.

SNAPSHOT: PROMISE

Liz is holding my hand. The credits for some children's show are playing in the background. It had been about good people and bad people, and it put bullying and being mean into very simple terms. Liz had reached for my hand, and now she asks me to promise with her to be good people forever. To never hurt anyone's feelings. To stand up for what is right, always.

I see the sincerity in her eyes, the faith that we can be heroes, so I agree.

CHAPTER TWENTY-TWO
Nevers and Forevers

Julia drives to the hospital with her eye on the gas gauge. The pointer is dipping uncomfortably close to E, and she doesn't have her credit card with her. Her wallet is still on her bed. She forgot to grab it when she left for the hospital yesterday afternoon, and she hadn't wanted to go home for it. Her father had left her a voicemail telling her exactly what he thought of her spending the night at the hospital, and she doesn't want him to know that she skipped school too.

Julia's relationship with her father is an estranged and rather bitter one. She blames him for his affair and the subsequent divorce, and besides, he is always disappointed in something. On the rare occasions when Julia looks back on her childhood, she only sees her shortcomings, because that was all anyone seemed to focus on. There was never a best, only better, and her greatest fear was always disappointing people.

Liz is afraid of silence, but Julia has long grown used to it. It's thicker in her house than in Liz's house—she avoids her father most nights, and he does nothing to change that. Julia is not entirely sure she wants him to. She has too many secrets, and so long as he doesn't pay attention, she can continue using his bank account.

Julia drives and tries not to think about that. She glances at her rearview mirror. Hanging from it is a pair of bouncy balls, hot glued together and tied with yarn, and Julia reaches for them.

They had gone skiing at a crappy little resort that was all that could be expected of anything within two hours of Meridian. The ski hill had looked stunted from the bottom but could have been Everest from the top, and try as she might, Julia simply hadn't been able to gather the will to lean forward and fall. Liz glanced at her face and, for once, kept quiet. They rode back down on the ski lift and left, and Liz waited until they had pulled out of the parking lot to start laughing.

"Grow a pair," she said as Julia coaxed her Ford Falcon onto the interstate.

Julia loved her car, which she had fondly nicknamed Mattie (short for Matilda) and everyone else had, less fondly, nicknamed Piece of Crap. She loved the way it smelled, like an old book with a hint of cigar smoke. She loved that it had a story, albeit one that the car dealer had refused to tell her. She hadn't minded—she made up a history of her own, one that included a rich Southern philanthropist and a short-lived love affair and an abandoned orange cat.

"First of my three wishes," Julia said drily. "Find me a lamp."

"Jem Hayden," Liz said immediately. "You can rub him—"

"Liz!"

"—of course he'd let you borrow his balls. Although," Liz said, pausing, "he might not be straight. I dunno, Jules. Doesn't he strike you as gay? A little bit? Has he tried to undress you yet?"

"Oh, my g—"

"He hasn't? He's gay. Jules, *I* can barely look at you without wanting to skip to third base."

The truth was that he *had* tried, and Julia had stopped him because she just wasn't sure. Everyone was pushing for her and Jem to hook up, because he was nice and smart and popular, and they would make an *adorable* couple. She couldn't see it. He was boring and always talked to her chest.

"God, Liz. Shut up."

The next week, Julia had found two bouncy balls waiting on her passenger seat, along with a note that said I GOT YOU A PAIR.

Julia smiled.

Sometimes it was difficult to like Liz Emerson. But it was very easy to love her.

Fifteen miles away from the crash site, Julia takes an exit ramp, because she's not sure she can drive past the crash site again. She can still see the Mercedes when she closes her eyes, and even though all of the mangled pieces will have been cleared away, she doesn't want to see it, the hill, the tree, the skid marks.

Julia forgets that Kennie is still at school, most likely looking for a ride to the hospital. She does not remember all the small comments Liz made to her in passing, that she thought funerals were stupid and that she didn't want people crying over her when she died. She can only think about how Liz was on this road yesterday, how the Mercedes was cruising down *this very road* in one piece yesterday. The passing cars, the blue ones—they could be the

Mercedes. One of them could hold Liz, whole and laughing. But if Julia passes the crash site, if she sees it, she can no longer pretend. Liz never made it past the tree, the hill.

Julia wonders where she had been going. The mall, maybe? But hadn't Liz been there just a few days ago?

With one tick mark away from E, she takes an exit and turns into McCraps (so christened in eighth grade with the introduction of snack wraps, which Liz had first called McWraps, and then McCraps after she tasted one; the name had eventually come to encompass the entire franchise). Julia parks and goes inside, and immediately the grease and noise and smell of meat envelop her. Her stomach rolls—Julia has been a vegetarian since fourth grade, ever since her class took a field trip to an organic farm. She had received a sloppy kiss from a calf and fallen in love, and when she learned on the bus back that it was destined to become hamburger, she swore to never eat meat again.

But what knocks the breath from her is this: the sizzling grease, the shouting. The old couple drinking coffee by the window, holding hands and smiling. The tired dad with triplets fighting over a pack of ketchup. The group of middle schoolers crowded in a booth, maybe skipping school for the first time ever, laughing.

She hates all of them.

For smiling. For laughing. For being well and unconcerned and happy while Liz is in the hospital with a ruptured lung and a broken leg and a shattered hand and too many internal injuries to keep track of. No one should be happy. The sun shouldn't be allowed to shine. The entire world should stay still for Liz Emerson.

It doesn't take a crash site to break Julia. What breaks her is a bit of noise, a few lights, and happiness.

She is on the floor without quite knowing how she got there, her knees pulled to her chest and her arms wrapped tightly around herself. Her eyes are shut, and in that darkness, she pretends to be alone. She says Liz's name, and then says it again and again until it blurs and becomes senseless between her lips, a spell too weak to make the world spin backward.

Liz.

Liz Liz Liz Liz Liz Liz Liz.

Soon she is surrounded by McCraps employees and the old couple and the dad and the triplets and the middle schoolers. Frantic voices, hands at her elbows. For a moment she is frightened—all these people staring, surely one of them will see the mistakes seeping through her skin, the yellowing teeth, the circles under her eyes, the trembling fingers.

But she buries herself deeper, and the memories rush

over her: all the times she, Liz, and Kennie snuck out to go to the best parties and the worst ones, all of the vastly insane things they did, all of the quiet afternoons spent in Liz's room painting their toenails while the TV mumbled in the background.

She thinks about how it is very, very unlikely that she, Liz, and Kennie will ever do anything like that ever again.

Nevers and forevers. These are Julia's greatest fears.

"I fell in love at a drive-through, honey," says the cheerful, fat manager who is driving Julia the rest of the way to the hospital. She had one of her employees fill Mattie up and drive behind them, and best of all, she didn't ask for an explanation when Julia asked her to avoid the interstate.

"He was my cashier. I ordered a Big Mac and paid with my heart. Ain't that the saddest thing you ever heard? Lemme tell you something, honey—men are goddamn terrified of babies. Fine. I'm goddamn terrified of commitment. And it ain't been easy, I tell you, but we ain't doing so bad, are we? We're keeping our heads up. . . ."

Julia does her best to listen. It's the least she can do, but while her heart slowly falls apart, the rest of her is restless. In the front right pocket of her backpack sits an almost-empty ziplock bag, and she grips the door handle so she can't reach for instant gratification, for escape.

In this moment, Julia would gladly have traded places with Liz, and she hates herself because of it.

Julia goes to the hospital.

Despite herself, she hopes.

She is vastly disappointed.

Liz is headed for surgery again. Sometime this morning, her heart had begun to stutter. Ten minutes ago, it began to fail. Now, she is wax beneath white lights and scalpels. Dr. Henderson is working over her, thinking about the note on her medical records: ORGAN DONOR. He thinks about that irony as he works. Liz Emerson will never donate her organs, because they are destroyed, and he doesn't know if they can get replacements soon enough.

It seems that Julia may have arrived just in time to see all of her fears come true.

CHAPTER TWENTY-THREE

Plans, New Year's Day

She took a nap on the brown couch with her arm flung over her eyes, and when she woke up with her suicide outlined backward across her cheek and HERE LIES LIZ EMERSON on her forehead, she continued to plan.

The party had not been the catalyst. Nor her stupidity. Nor her hands all over the hot torso of the boy who had gotten Kennie pregnant. It wasn't the anger that clawed her insides to shreds, anger at all the idiocy, anger at the world, anger that made her dig her nails into Kyle's skin even as her lips were on his.

No, the party was simply the last straw.

She had been desperate to feel something, anything. She

needed a window, because she had broken her heart throwing it at locked doors.

Liz got up off the brown couch. She looked down and saw a natural disaster. She could not exist without tearing everything around her to shreds.

Over the next two weeks, Liz Emerson drafted her plans and revised them. She did her research and made sure she would have enough money to pay for gas and set a date.

And she also gave herself a way out.

A week—that's what she allowed herself. An entire week before the last day. She thought of Julia filling herself up and Kennie becoming empty, and she understood. Life was precious. She knew that, knew it deeply, so she would try again. She would try what she tried on the night of the party, but she would do it right this time. Seven days, seven chances. She would wake up seven more times and search again for a reason to go on. She would give the entire world a week to change her mind.

But she also knew that life was fragile, and if her week failed, she knew how to shatter.

CHAPTER TWENTY-FOUR

Seven Days Before Liz Emerson Crashed Her Car

Most of the varsity girls played in the winter indoor soccer league, because Julia's father had offered to pay for everyone this year as part of his annual attempt to mend his relationship with his daughter. They were all drained from the pre-calc test, and the atmosphere in the locker room was quieter than usual. The team they were playing today was made up of girls from a Division One school. They knew today's game would be a train wreck.

As everyone else adjusted their shin guards and did last-minute stretches, Liz sat on the bench and looked around at each of them, and realized that she had spent the last seven years of her life with these girls and knew no more than the most superficial details about them. Jenna Haverick was great with headers and had a dog named Napoleon. Skyler Matthews was right-handed but played with her left foot, and only ate butter pecan ice cream. Allison Chevero was great at making fouls look accidental, and she had a tramp stamp that her parents still didn't know about.

Other than Julia, these girls were worse than strangers. These were people she had spent years and years with and never even wondered about. She had never asked about their fears or failures, successes and embarrassments. She just didn't *care* very much, and as she sat on the bench with her team around her, the absolute sadness of the fact overwhelmed her. She knew so many people, so many, but what was the point? How many of them did she really care about? How many of them really cared about her?

"Liz?"

She looked up. Julia was standing beside her, frowning slightly as she pulled her hair into a high ponytail. Right then, Liz had never been so grateful for Julia, had never felt so guilty as she stared at the dark circles beneath Julia's eyes.

Julia saw it. She sat down and said nothing, only waited. She gave Liz a choice.

Liz, unfortunately, chose wrong.

There were just too many things she wanted to say to Julia. She wanted to apologize for a thousand things. She wanted to tell her how desperately thankful she was for her and Kennie. She wanted to say that she could never ask for better friends, but all of those things sounded stupid in her head, so instead, she got to her feet and said, "Come on. Let's go kick some ass."

There was some cheering and hollering from the rest of the team in response, and they left the locker room together. But then some of the girls peeled off to go grab their water bottles and other ones had to retrieve bobby pins and hair ties, and by the time Liz reached the field, only a fraction of her team remained.

Coach Gilson frowned when he saw them. "Where is everyone?"

"Coming," said Liz, but the word caught in her throat. An odd unhappiness rose inside her when she said it, because she was once again making promises that she had no power to keep.

Eventually, though, the team did regroup. The referee flipped the coin and the girls got into their positions, and Liz tried to focus on the game.

But there was something terrifying taking over her thoughts, and it wouldn't leave. Out of the seven billion people sharing the planet with her, not one of them knew what was going through her head. Not one of them knew that she was lost. Not one of them asked.

The whistle blew.

Usually, soccer allowed her to forget. She fell in love with the sport because of the way it consumed her, swallowed her whole, grabbed all her attention and stored it in a sphere that they chased and kicked and passed between them like a secret. She obsessed over the unpredictability. She was wholly addicted to the adrenaline.

Once, a yearbook reporter had asked Liz to describe her favorite part of soccer. What came to her mind was this: the moment when her foot connected with the ball at the perfect angle, with exactly enough force and just the right timing. It was a rare thing, and it was from those exceedingly rare moments that her weird zeal for soccer took root and grew into something immense. She got this feeling of *rightness* after every beautiful pass, every soaring shot. She could never exactly describe it, but it reminded her of snapping the last piece of a puzzle into place or pushing a key into a lock, of being utterly certain, somehow, that *this was it*. In those moments, the world held its breath and everything fit, and she stood in the middle of it all, knowing.

During the interview, however, what she said was this: "Winning."

In this game, neither happened.

They were righteously slaughtered. The first half was downright embarrassing. When they went back to the locker room at halftime, the scoreboard flashed 4-0 at their backs.

They were getting desperate by the time they gave up another goal five minutes into the second half, Liz especially. She had wanted today to be the one to change her mind. She had hoped to have one of those connecting moments, to look around and remember that the world made sense, that some things fell apart so better things could fall together.

But her passes were messy and all of her shots went wide.

Within the first ten minutes of the second half, the team had received six yellow cards. Ellen Baseny got a red card for telling the referee to fuck himself, and two fans were ejected for mooning.

Liz went in for a goal. They were down 5-1 now with two minutes left, and she knew it was a lost cause. Who cared? She was a lost cause, and she was trying, wasn't she?

One of the defenders from the other team muttered, "Don't miss again, skank."

Then she laughed.

And Liz aimed for her instead.

Had the defender been familiar with Liz Emerson's

reputation, she would have kept her mouth shut. Not just Liz's reputation as a person, but also her reputation of having the hardest kick in the state.

The defender was rushed to the emergency room.

Liz was given a yellow card. The referee decided that Liz hadn't meant to do it—she *had* been trying to score, after all, and the defender had been in the way.

And Liz Emerson got away with one more thing.

The final whistle sounded, but she stayed on the field for a while. She looked around the fluorescent dome, at the cleat marks on the grass, and she didn't want to move. She was so tired. She didn't want to move ever again.

Eventually, though, she went to the locker room to peel off her sweaty jersey, prepared to go home and maybe dig around in her mother's wine cabinet and take a few shots on the white couch. But when she got there, everyone was laughing.

"Damn, Liz, you freaking *pegged her.* Dude, that was *amazing.*"

"*Surgery.* The bitch has to get *surgery.*"

"Hell, yeah. She deserves it."

It made her sick. Liz closed her eyes for a moment as she shoved everything back into her bag. God. What had she been thinking? She couldn't even remember. It had been plain stupid, and not just that, it had been cruel. The other girl would have to pay for surgery, physical therapy, and she'd definitely be sitting out the season.

Liz imagined the situation being reversed. She imagined missing the entire season, not even having soccer to take her mind off things—

Liz walked out of the sports club and stood in the frigid air. She felt a bead of sweat freeze as it made its way down her spine, and she tilted her head back to look at the sky and asked, *Why?*

Then she got into her car, and on her way home, it struck her that she hadn't signed up as an organ donor. She hadn't wanted to when she got her license—her body was *hers*. She slammed her brakes and turned sharply, flipped off the guy who beeped, and headed for the local clinic.

Five minutes later, the clipboard of paperwork lay in her lap. Her fingers were wrapped tightly around the pen, and her eyes were closed. In her head, she made a list. It was titled *Things I've Done Right*, and this was the first item.

In a week, she thought, *I will have two.*

And my heart will beat for someone who deserves it.

CHAPTER TWENTY-FIVE

Driving Habits

"*G*od, Mom," snaps Kennie. "Why don't you drive even slower?"

"I'm already driving two miles above the speed limit, Kennie."

Kennie is fairly certain that her mother is the only person alive who has ever been ticketed for driving too *slowly*—it had happened during freshman year; she was late to school, and even the office ladies had laughed at her, the bitches—which makes her all the more upset that Julia had totally ditched her, that her mom wouldn't let her drive to the hospital with Carly Blake.

Liz.

"I could have driven myself," says Kennie.

"In light of recent events, I don't think that would have been a good idea."

And she begins to lecture again, her favorite rant, all statistics about car accidents and insurance, and Kennie ignores her as usual. She looks out the window and searches for signs of the crash.

She doesn't know exactly where it was—Facebook wasn't specific, but she searches and figures that, somewhere along the way, she will find it. She has to see it. She has to see the spot that defeated Liz Emerson, because part of her still refuses to believe it exists.

And just then, she sees it.

A splintered fence, ruined snow all around. She doesn't look twice—can't, because her eyes have filled and the world has blurred. A sob is building, and Kennie grips her seat with both of her hands.

". . . and Liz was a lovely girl, of course, but her driving has always worried me. I can't say I'm entirely surprised, honey—"

Kennie whirls. "Mom!" she screams. *"Just stop!"*

"Kendra Ann! I'm trying to teach you to have good driving habits. You need to learn some responsibility, and that temper of yours! You need to have a meeting with Pastor Phil for—"

"I don't care," says Kennie. *"I do not care."*

Her mother snaps something back, but Kennie has started crying. She really doesn't care, not at all, doesn't care about anything except the fact that the fence is broken and the snow is dirty, and yesterday in that spot, her best friend nearly died.

She is so busy crying that she doesn't see the actual crash site when they pass it.

Good thing too. I don't think Kennie could have handled it. If a broken fence from a rogue cow and a patch of trampled snow could push her into screaming at her mother—or rather, made her so terrified that she stopped after screaming that one line—maybe it was lucky that she didn't see the contorted tree, the little scraps of blue Mercedes, the snow still streaked with pink.

"She *is*," Kennie whispers to herself.

She is *a lovely girl.*

CHAPTER TWENTY-SIX

Forty-Nine Minutes Before Liz Emerson Crashed Her Car

*T*he answer was *breaking.*

Her childhood ended on the day she watched Melody's feet dangle, and maybe she hadn't realized it then, but what she decided was this: she would no longer be an object at rest. The only other option was to be what Mackenzie was. An object in motion that would stay in motion, even if it meant flattening everything in her path.

And so she broke every promise she had ever made. And with the energy from so many shattered things, she pushed herself into motion.

CHAPTER TWENTY-SEVEN

Twenty-Three Missed Calls Later

"*M*om? Yeah, I—okay, yeah, I'm sorry. I fell asleep—

"No, I'm not drunk, Mom. I'm not high, either—yeah, sure, I'd be happy to bring home some of my pee in a coffee cup, if you don't care if it spills. I'm driving your car. Seriously, I'm—

"Mom. Mom. *Mom.*

"Yeah, I *know* you called me twenty-three times. . . . I can see it on my phone—no, it died while I was asleep, I brought my charger—well, I couldn't see it then, could I? I don't sleep with my eyes open—okay, yeah, sorry, Mom. I—no, I don't think aggression is a side effect of meth. Steroids, maybe—*I'm not on steroids.*

"I'm at—no, I'm not interrupting you—do you want me to answer that? I'm at the hospital—

"I'M FINE.

"No, I have not overdosed.

"No, I don't have alcohol poisoning.

"Mom, just listen—I'm here for a . . . classmate . . . no, you don't know her—she's not *pregnant*! I don't have a girl-friend. No, I didn't have sex last night—I wish—kidding, *kidding*. Chill. I'm fine.

"She got into a car accident. I saw her car on my way to Costco—well, I didn't move it, so I assume your purse is still in the car, unless someone broke a window and stole it—no one broke a window, Mom. Yeah, I'll check later. Okay, I have to go—no, because people are starting to stare at me like I'm insane. Yeah, there are other kids from school here too—they're all just getting here, school must have let out . . . no, I didn't, I told you, I was asleep. I didn't *skip,* Mom, I . . . overslept a bit. Yeah, pretty much. Until like, one thirty. I haven't slept in ages, Mom. I was up until three the night before last night working on that stupid physics project. . . . Okay. Yeah, I'll come home tonight. . . . Yeah, I know. I know. Sorry. *Sorry.* Yeah, okay. Love you too."

CHAPTER TWENTY-EIGHT
The On-Again-Off-Again

Jake Derrick has not come to see Liz Emerson.

Liam realizes this after he hangs up with his mother and looks around. The waiting room resembles the high school during lunch hour. The cafeteria has a distinctive seating arrangement: the center tables belong to the popular, the outer rings to the nerds and outcasts and dorks and freshmen. Here in the waiting room, the jockiest and the preppiest, the ones who knew Liz the best, have taken over the center area with an air of manifest destiny.

Liam is still beside the window, undoubtedly the least popular person in the room.

But from his position, it's easy to see everyone who comes

and goes, and Liam is certain that Liz's boyfriend has yet to arrive. It takes him a moment to remember whether or not they are, in fact, still together. Jake and Liz had established their tumultuous relationship at the end of Liz's freshman year, and Liam has paid attention without meaning to. He can't help it. His crush on Liz Emerson began on the first day of fifth grade, and except for the year or so during which he had hated her guts, he has paid attention.

No. Even then.

But the truth is, *everyone* pays attention. That's why they were all here last night; that's why they're all here now. She is Liz Emerson. She matters.

To everyone, it seems, except her boyfriend.

It started when Jake kissed her under the stars in the movie theater parking lot. He was a grade ahead of her, had made the varsity football team in his freshman year, and was widely lusted after. That night, he literally swept her off her feet. According to popular opinion, it was the most romantic thing that had happened all year. According to Liz, it was the definition of cliché, and he had tasted of nacho cheese.

Their most infamous breakup had taken place during sophomore year. It was the night of the homecoming game, and Liz dumped Jake right after he made the winning touchdown.

On the way to some party—Liz hadn't even been sure whose it was, but it had alcohol and pot and people, so it didn't matter, they were going—she told Julia and Kennie, "God, he's just one big cliché."

Jake Derrick is. He is decently hot but not nearly as hot as he thinks, and only about half as funny. He is not quite as stupid as everyone assumes, remains blissfully and utterly unaware of his own supreme arrogance, and will never, ever deserve Liz.

And certainly Liam is jealous, but he dislikes Jake because Liam is one of the few people who have paid attention closely enough to know that Liz does not like Jake either.

Liz and Jake's favorite pastime is fighting. Jake is the kind of person who is absolutely assured of his own rightness, and Liz is the kind of person whose primary goal in life is to tear such people down. Their fights involved Jake calling Liz unmentionable things and Liz snapping back with comments that hurt where only she knew to hurt him.

Three days before Liz crashed her car, they started arguing about Liz's physics project on gravity. Liz was almost done, and Jake was trying to make her feel stupid by saying some shit about how acceleration is the third derivative of position and telling her to change everything, and it turned nasty very quickly.

Eventually Jake called Liz a bitch and told her to fuck off and go to hell all in one breath, and Liz had laughed in his face and slammed the door behind him.

Liam does not know about the fight. He has no access to the best gossip, and it always takes awhile for news to trickle down to his lowly position among the other nerds and rejects.

It is true, however, that despite the fight, Liz and Jake never actually broke up. Technically. In the end, Liz simply did not want to waste any more time on Jake, even to dump him. She was searching for a reason to live, and he wasn't helping.

As much as Liam dislikes Jake Derrick, it disgusts him that he is not here. Jake and Liz have been a couple for nearly three years. He should be here, at least, pretending to be heartbroken.

Or maybe Jake really would have been heartbroken. Liam doesn't know. He doesn't know Jake well and has no particular wish to remedy that situation, so he makes a halfhearted attempt to withhold judgment.

But the truth is that Jake Derrick's heart is a fickle and

melodramatic thing. He has teared up over dead dogs and spectacular football games, and no doubt he will cry over Liz too. But in a month, two, he will be making out with another girl, someone with bigger boobs who will believe him when he lies. Liz will become no more than a pickup line.

"I fell in love in high school. I know that's cliché and stuff, but it's true—Liz and I had something real. When she died, I just . . . I don't know. I was so lost. Maybe I still am. I'm lost."

CHAPTER TWENTY-NINE
Scavenger

*L*iz only stayed with Jake for so long because he kept something inside her alive, some piece of her that still believed in love and yearned for romance. And he could be so sweet, so adorable in the things he did, sending her flowers with notes written on the petals, sneaking up behind her in the hallway to bury his face in her hair, telling her all the time that she was beautiful, that she took his breath away.

Then there was homecoming during junior year, just a few months before. Liz was about to break up with him once and for all, and then he did something that made her wonder about love again.

△▽△

She opened her locker after her last class, and a flower fell out. There was a ribbon tied around the stem, and some sort of Shakespeare quote written on it in Jake's scrawl, which should have turned her off right away. Julia liked Shakespeare. Liz liked the cynics—Orwell, Twain, Swift, Hemingway. But she had just come from the homecoming pep rally; the hallways were loud and her hair was messy from the wind and the flower and ribbon were so beautiful that in that moment, she felt beautiful too.

IT IS THE EAST, AND LIZ IS THE SUN, the ribbon said (and truthfully, a part of Liz cringed because Jake was just so goddamn cliché). GO EAST, SUNSHINE, TO THE PLACE WHERE WE FIRST MET.

So she did. She went to the middle school, about three hundred feet east of the high school. The first time she had ever talked to Jake had been sixth grade. They had arrived at the water fountain by the gym at the same time, and he had gallantly stepped back. For a moment, she thought it was incredibly sweet that he had remembered, but as she walked toward the middle school, a twinge of suspicion grew inside her. Jake was not the sentimental type—he could hardly remember what had happened last week, much less what had happened five years ago.

She went into the building and stopped in front of the

water fountain by the gym, read the waiting card. YOUR LIPS ON MINE, UNDER THE STARS. At the movie theater parking lot, she picked up the waiting teddy bear and took the note from its paws: WHERE WE HAD OUR FIRST DATE, A TEA PARTY WITH TEDDY BEARS. The hospital, where she had visited him after he had broken his collarbone playing football. She had brought him a mug of chai tea (which Jake had ignored in favor of his hospital-issued chili dog) and a get-well bear as a joke. They had ended up making out in the hospital bed until a nurse had come and asked Liz, none too politely, to leave.

The scavenger hunt led her all over Meridian and wasted an entire tank of gas, and at the end, she found herself parked at the edge of the overgrown field by the elementary school. Jake was standing in the middle of it, holding a sign with the last clue written in black Sharpie.

It said WILL YOU GO TO THE DANCE WITH ME?

She said yes.

Liz had a generally hard time believing in love, and she was not in love with Jake Derrick. She was in love with the things he did. Turned out, though, her suspicions were correct—the scavenger hunt was beyond the imagination of her self-involved boyfriend. Jake had known that Liz's friends would do the majority of the work. Really, all he had to do was stand there.

But that afternoon, in the abandoned field by the elementary school, Liz pretended that they were. In love. She lied to herself. Her world was almost beautiful. She didn't care that it was false.

CHAPTER THIRTY

After the Surgery

There are three kinds of people after the surgery is pronounced successful.

There are the ones who are breathless, shaking, crying in that crushing and desperate kind of relief—namely, Liz's mother and Julia. When the doctor first told Monica that her daughter had not died on the operating table, she went to Julia and held her, because she couldn't hold Liz.

All team practices have been cancelled for the day, so the waiting room is clogged with the second kind of people, the ones who aren't surprised at all. They shrug and say that they were never worried, never mind the fact that they had all abandoned their homework out of their professed concern. They sit around the low tables and say that they always knew Liz was strong enough to pull through.

And then there is Matthew Derringer, who is just the slightest bit disappointed, because he has already ordered flowers for the funeral.

CHAPTER THIRTY-ONE
The Art of Being Alive

*J*ulia has always been the good girl, Sunday afternoon activities aside. So her heart is nearly falling out of her chest when she grabs a pair of scrubs from a passing cart, pulls them over her jeans, and walks into the ICU with all the nonchalance she can muster.

It smells clean, clean like linens and antiseptics, like organized and monitored death. There are rows and rows of almost-corpses buried beneath white sheets. Julia has never shied away from blood or sickness, but this room makes her want to run and never look back. She doesn't want to see Liz here.

But she does. As always, Liz Emerson is hard to miss.

This time, it's because, of all the patients, Liz looks furthest from reanimation. She looks beyond hope.

Julia's legs are shaking as she walks over to Liz's bed. She stops a good six feet away, afraid to go any closer, afraid that she will bump into one of the many machines and something will unhook and Liz will die and it will be her fault.

There is a chair by Liz's head, and Julia stares at it for a long while before she decides to sit down. She slides her backpack from her shoulder, takes out a pre-calc textbook, and opens it to the chapter the class is studying.

She begins to read. I watch her lips move. They're trembling too.

"'For any point on an ellipse, the sum value of the distances from any given point to each foci will be a fixed value.' I remember this chapter. Don't worry. The test is easier than the homework, and she'll probably curve the quiz. You won't miss much. Anyway. 'In the case of a hyperbola, however, the difference between the distances will be . . .'"

Julia glances down at Liz's face and begins to cry. She had tried to avoid it, looking, but it's terribly difficult to not look at an almost-corpse, when the almost-corpse is your best friend.

Liz's face is gray like air pollution. Her hair is a mess, and parts of it have been chopped off so the doctors could stitch up her scalp. There are shadows beneath her eyes and bruises all over one cheek, and worst of all, her eyes are closed.

Liz has always hated sleeping. Once, we read the story of Sleeping Beauty together—we didn't understand much, because it was a harder version, and an unhappier one. Everyone was dead by the time the princess woke up, and maybe that was when Liz began to fear missing things.

The makeup is gone and her face is as naked as Julia has ever seen it. She sees the sadness, the exhaustion, the fault lines beneath the surface, and suddenly Julia is furious. If Liz had slept more, maybe she would have been a more careful driver. Maybe she wouldn't have been so reckless and ruthless and lost.

A tear slides down Julia's nose and falls onto Liz's hand. Julia watches her face for a sign of life. For anything.

But Liz is motionless, a girl of wax and shadows.

"Damn you," Julia whispers, her voice small. "We were supposed to go running tonight. Open gym for soccer starts next week."

They would have gone too—Liz liked running through snow. She would go now, were her leg not broken in three places.

Well, maybe not.

For soccer, Liz almost waited. The chances of Meridian's girls' varsity soccer team winning the state tournament have gone down dramatically. Without their junior captain and star forward, it will be a miracle if they even pass sectionals, and Liz hadn't wanted to be responsible for that failure too.

But she needed ice on the roads. She needed her accident to look as accidental as possible.

And she just didn't think she was capable of waiting another three months.

Julia, however, knows none of this. She looks down at what remains of her best friend, and she thinks of all the times Liz was quiet and not really there. The times when she was the Liz everyone else knows, all snark and insanity, and the moments when she was the one that stared at invisible things and hadn't truly smiled in a long time.

"God, Liz," Julia says, and she closes her eyes to force the tears back. They overflow anyway, pooling somewhere deep inside her. "I can't run in the rain alone."

It was right before cross-country season, junior year. It was pouring outside, and Julia was curled on the window seat with a book and a cup of soup when someone began ringing her doorbell insistently. She opened the front door and found Liz standing on her porch in nothing but a pair of rain-soaked shorts and an obnoxiously green sports bra.

"Come on," said Liz. "Let's go running."

Julia gaped. "What the hell are you—it's raining!"

"I've noticed," Liz said impatiently. "Go change." She looked at Julia's chest critically. "You'll start an earthquake if you let those things bounce."

"Liz, it's *wet.*"

"No shit, Sherlock. Now *come on.*"

Julia closed the door in Liz's face and waited to see if Liz would leave.

She didn't, of course, so Julia went upstairs to change into a sports bra and her Nikes.

And they went running.

The rain was warm and smelled of beginnings. Liz and Julia ran unevenly, their footsteps syncopated: right right foot, left left foot. After a few minutes, Julia fell back a bit, because her strides were longer than Liz's—it was kind of awkward trying to run beside her, because she had to take a normal step, and then a smaller one so that Liz could match it—and she was already wheezing. Breathing in the contents of ziplock bags did nothing to improve her lung capacity.

But Liz didn't say anything and didn't care that she wheezed, and Julia was thankful.

She closed her eyes and threw her head back. The rain hit her face and slid down her shoulders. Her legs were muddy and her shoes were so heavy with water that they released a small wave with every step. She just ran, and there was something eloquent in the sound of rain and footsteps.

"Watch it, gimp," Liz said when Julia veered into her. Julia's eyes snapped back open, and she found Liz running backward and smirking at her, and Julia laughed because she loved the ache in her legs, the stretch in her muscles, the heavy thudding of her heart, the rain that was everywhere.

She failed to notice that the wetness on Liz's face wasn't rain. She didn't realize that Liz was drowning, or that Liz was crying because she knew that she could never outrun the things she had done.

"Where are we going?" Julia asked, but Liz didn't answer. Julia was okay with that. Liz rarely ran the same route twice, and Julia didn't mind following.

So they just ran, and eventually they turned a corner and Julia saw Barry's Pond, which a disgustingly rich old couple from Florida had recently purchased. It had been a controversial sale—Meridian generally disproved of outsiders. Julia slowed as the grass turned to sand, but Liz went faster. Julia opened her mouth to say "What the hell," but before she could, Liz ran onto the dock and over the edge without stopping, and disappeared in a flurry of bubbles.

"Crap," Julia said under her breath, and then, louder, "Liz?"

But Liz didn't come up, and after a minute, Julia began to panic. It was raining harder now, and she could hardly see. She ran onto the dock and stood at the edge, waiting for Liz to pop up, but she didn't.

"Liz!" Julia shouted, bending over the water. "Liz—!"

Then she screamed, clear and shrill, as Liz shot out of the water, grabbed her, and dragged her under.

Julia came up choking. Liz was choking too, because she had been laughing as she pulled Julia into the water. Julia wanted to snap about fifty things at Liz as she coughed the water out of her lungs, but as she turned to, she saw Liz laughing and breathless and brilliant and beautiful and hers.

So she splashed her.

Liz splashed her back, and they chased each other through the pond and the rain, their heads thrown back to drink in the sky, their fingers wrinkled, their hair plastered to their scalps.

Eventually, they dragged themselves back onto the dock to lie in the rain, which had faded into a drizzle. It tickled and left behind a fogginess that made the world blurry at the edges and just for them, only them.

As Julia lay there, her eyes closed, the splintering dock digging into her back in a dozen places, she heard Liz say quietly, "Thanks for coming with me."

Julia smiled and sighed an unintelligible response. She spread her arms wide and felt the elastic of her sports bra tightening with every inhale, and for a moment, she couldn't feel where she ended and the world began.

"I love you guys," Liz said suddenly, fiercely. "You and Kennie. God, I don't know what I'd do without you two."

Julia opened her eyes. Liz was lying beside her, her bare stomach rising and falling very slightly. Her hair had fallen out of its ponytail and framed her face like a nest, and suddenly Julia was afraid, because Liz, her Liz, always kept her heart locked away.

"Are you drunk?" she asked, uncertainly.

"No," Liz said, and she smiled.

Julia had seen Liz in homecoming dresses and in pajamas, Ralph Lauren blazers and flip-flops from Target, but she had never seen Liz as beautiful as she was then, with her eyes closed and her lips just barely, barely curved, because until then, Julia had never associated the word *peaceful* with Liz Emerson.

Liz sighed. It was a soundless thing, only a parting of lips. "Sometimes," she said, so softly that Julia wasn't sure if she was meant to hear, "sometimes I forget that I'm alive."

So, in the hospital, looking over an utterly different Liz, one who looks everything except peaceful, Julia leans forward and whispers two words to her, suddenly, fiercely.

"You're alive."

CHAPTER THIRTY-TWO

Six Days Before Liz Emerson Crashed Her Car

*I*t was one of those quiet days, muted somehow, lit by a fuzzy sun behind thin clouds. Liz had finished all of her homework in study hall and the school had ordered Jimmy John's for lunch, and—well, maybe she was too numb to be content, but six days before she crashed her car, Liz Emerson was no unhappier than usual.

Until she went home, and things began to go downhill.

Liz had just unlocked the door when Kennie called.

Liz answered the phone and Kennie's voice screamed, "Oh my god, just leave me alone, Mom!" A door slammed, and Kennie said into the phone, "Hi. I can't go shopping. My mom's being a bitch. Surprise."

"What did you do this time?" Liz's voice bounced from wall to wall. *Damn house,* she thought, and promised herself that she would never buy a big house. And laughed, because here was a promise she could keep.

"It's not funny," Kennie snapped. "I didn't do anything to her. I'm not done with that stupid physics project, and I keep telling my mom that it isn't due until next Wednesday, but she says I need to stop procrastinating and get, like, an attitude adjustment. It's not like it's even my fault, 'cause fucking Carly Blake won't actually touch *our* project—*What, Mom?*"

The door slammed again. "Anyway. Yeah. Sorry." When Liz didn't say anything, Kennie said, "Ask Julia. Her dad doesn't care where she is, does he?"

Which was unkind, especially coming from Kennie. They didn't talk about Julia's dad, just like they didn't talk about Kennie's mom or Liz's pre-Meridian life. Liz didn't comment, however, because she knew how much Kennie hated it when her mom nagged and nosed. She'd been like this since the abortion—snapping and cynical, and the personality fit her like a sweater that had shrunk in the wash. But then Liz thought she would be too, and then she thought, *Don't think, not that, not today, don't think.*

"Julia's still at Zero," she said.

That was what they called O'Hare University, the local

college. University O, zero, and where most of them would end up after they graduated. Julia took analytic geometry (which was abbreviated on her transcripts as Anal. Geo., a fact that Kennie usually found endlessly funny) and health physics there, because Meridian High didn't offer them and because Julia was a goddamn try-hard.

"Oh. Okay," sighed Kennie. "I should go. Sorry. Maybe next week."

Or not.

Liz hung up without saying anything, and now she was stuck with the silence. It magnified, the silence—Liz was annoyed after she hung up, but within minutes, she was truly and unapologetically pissed off at Kennie, at Kennie's mother, and she threw in the rest of the world for the hell of it.

It took three seconds to decide that she couldn't stay in the house for the rest of the day, so she shoved her feet into running shoes and went out the garage door. The winter was a wall that she smacked straight into, the air a living thing that crawled through her sweats and layers and settled against her skin.

Liz had always loved the cold. When she was younger, she loved breathing in and feeling her snot freeze, and she never grew out of it. She put her iPod on shuffle and slid it into her pocket, and she began to run.

Sometimes she ran just to take wrong turns and different routes, because she liked getting lost. But the truth was, Liz hated running. She did it to stay in shape for soccer or to get out of the house, but she would never play a soccer game again and the house would still be there when she got back.

But she always felt like she was chasing something when she ran, something invisible that she never caught. It felt like she was playing tag with herself, and Liz hated tag.

She ran the mile loop around her house and ran it again, and as she started the third mile, she could barely breathe and her entire body was cramping. She was tired of seeing all of the same things over and over again; she was tired of running in circles. She didn't want to chase anymore.

This is stupid.

I should stop.

So she did.

Fuck running, she thought. *Fuck tag.*

She went inside and slammed the door behind her. Then she opened it and slammed it again, slammed it and slammed it harder. She put all of her weight into it and the force was so great that one of the vases fell off the mantle and shattered, spitting crystal across the wood and chipping the polish. She ignored it and went upstairs and slammed her own door.

Overreacting, she told herself, and her own anger frightened her, but not enough to calm down. She tried, though—really she did. She shoved a superhero movie into her Blu-ray player and went straight to the scene in which the hero made his final stand and the background music was so dramatic and soaring that it always made her cry. But today everything was cut from cardboard, and a minute later, she was ripping the movie out, breaking it in half, fourths, throwing the pieces across the room.

She grabbed her camera and hurled it at the wall. It smashed to pieces after making a dent in the plaster. She could feel all of her little cracks widening into larger ones, faults that ran all through her, tore her apart. She took the old, worn books from her bookshelf and ripped them in half, one by one; the pages fluttered around her as she reached for the rest of the movies, all the stupid heroes, and broke them all.

She struck her lamp off her desk and shredded her homework. She hurled her calculator at the floor and flung a perfume bottle at the mirror. The mirror stayed intact, but the bottle shattered, flooding her vanity with perfume and glass.

Her breath caught in her throat. She took a step back and looked around her room, and an odd feeling rose within her. It always did, when she was staring at shattered things—an urge to get to her hands and knees and gather them to her. She wanted to stack them back together and make them whole again.

But she couldn't, and so she sat down in the center of her room with all those pieces spreading around her, and made a wish instead.

I wish second chances were real.

SNAPSHOT: WISHES

Liz is leaning over the edge of the tower. I am holding her hand and her father hovers behind her, and together we keep her steady. She looks down and makes a wish on the dandelion she has gripped in her small, sweaty hand the entire way up. She wishes for the only thing she has ever wished for.

Liz Emerson wishes to fly.

After, she'll look at me and tell me to make a wish too.

Years later, she will remember all those wishes. She will consider jumping off that very tower to see if any of them came true.

In the end, she will decide against it. She won't know how to make jumping off a scenic tower look like an accident.

CHAPTER THIRTY-THREE

Worlds Fall Apart

*K*ennie doesn't arrive at the hospital until after the commotion has mostly died down. "God, Mom, no one else's parents are here," she snaps as she gets out of the car, because despite everything, she's still afraid of how her mother's appearance will affect what people think of her. She knows it's despicable, but she can't help it.

And part of her is afraid because she had her abortion not far from here, and doctors all knew each other, right?

"Maybe you should stay in the car, Mom," she says. But her mother insists on coming in, so Kennie runs ahead.

She stops at the entrance and looks up at the great blur of a building through her tears. It's very unreal to her that

Liz, *Liz*, is behind one of those windows, barely alive.

Her mother comes up behind her and fusses a bit over the state of Kennie's hair and makeup. Maybe this is why she has always been so preoccupied with what people think of her—because her parents always are. Appearances matter in her household, and Kennie has grown up with the impression that she is only what people think she is.

Kennie swats at her mother and runs, toward Liz and away from the rest of it.

She bursts into the waiting room and everyone surrounds her, hugs and tissues while her mom goes to talk to Liz's mom, and then,

"Heart."

"Failing."

"Almost died."

"Where were you?"

"No," says Kennie when her mother, who has left Monica, tries to comfort her. Their mothers don't like each other, which is fine—Kennie doesn't like her mother right now either. "No, just stop. *Stop*."

But someone else tries to take her place. "*No!*" she screams blindly, her eyes shut to all of them. "Go away, just leave me alone—*leave me alone!*"

She slides to the ground, and the tears come.

△▽△

When Julia finally takes off the scrubs and makes her way back to the waiting room, Kennie is the first person she sees.

She sits in a corner sobbing great, heaving sobs, curled into herself as though she could disappear, her hair fanning and frizzing over her shoulders. Strangest of all, she is alone. Julia watches a moment, and then it hits her that she has been a terrible friend. She walks over slowly, the sounds of her approach drowned out by Kennie's great gasps, and crouches down beside her.

"Kennie . . ."

Kennie raises her face a fraction of an inch, and Julia gets a glimpse of the mess of mascara and red eyes.

"Y-you didn't tell me," Kennie blubbers. "Y-y-you didn't even c-call me."

Julia bites her lip and swallows hard. "I'm sorry. Kennie, I just—I'm so sorry. I just . . . I forgot. I'm sorry."

"And you left me at school," Kennie says with a muffled wail.

Julia can only nod, because she doesn't think she has ever felt this guilty.

Then Kennie is bawling all over Julia's sweatshirt. Julia puts her arms around Kennie's thin shoulders and leans her cheek against Kennie's arm. They sit there for a small eternity. This is their pain, their tragedy, because Liz is theirs.

"Have you s-seen her?" Kennie finally whispers into Julia's shoulder.

Julia nods again.

"Is she . . . how is she?"

Broken. Dying. Unfixable. Gone.

Julia says, "Sleeping."

Kennie buries her face deeper in Julia's sweatshirt, and Julia holds her tighter.

CHAPTER THIRTY-FOUR

Forty-Four Minutes Before Liz Emerson
Crashed Her Car

*L*iz thought about Kennie.

Kennie always acted so shallow that sometimes it was difficult to remember that she wasn't.

At the end of seventh grade, Kennie had bought the three of them matching rings with BFFS engraved inside the band. They were cheesy, cheap things that later turned their fingers green, and on those rings, they swore proportionally cheesy, cheap promises: that they would always be there for each other. They would remember each other's shortcomings and they would fill them. They would do the "all for one and one for all" thing, forever.

Kennie's greatest shortcoming was her inability to say

no, and Liz knew that. Everyone knew that.

And so, forty-four minutes before she crashed her car, Liz thought about how Kennie had done everything Liz had ever told her to—or tried, at least—and how Liz had never once told Kennie to do the right thing. She thought about all the parties at which she had seen Kennie giggling and drunk in the arms of almost-strangers, all the parties at which Liz had watched different boys lead Kennie into different bedrooms. She could clearly remember too many instances when Kennie had glanced back with a sort of helpless look in her eyes, and Liz had only laughed and called Kennie a slut in a loving way, and turned away because she wanted to keep drinking and dancing and forgetting.

CHAPTER THIRTY-FIVE

Five Days Before Liz Emerson Crashed Her Car

She promised herself, once, that she would never puke again.

It started during the summer before seventh grade, when she and Kennie looked in the mirror while trying on swimsuits and called themselves fat. Liz had decided to eat less, less still, and then not at all. She told Kennie to do it with her, and Kennie had tried, but she wasn't very good at it. Kennie loved food more than she loved being skinny. She went on and off, sneaking food when she said she wasn't eating, stashing it in her room. Liz thought that their little diet might have made Kennie eat even more than she used to, but it didn't matter—Kennie didn't gain a pound. Lucky Kennie.

Liz, of course, didn't last much longer. She liked eating too. Bulimia was her compromise, and what a deal it was. Eat all you want, gain nothing. It was perfect, until she started playing soccer again in the spring of seventh grade, and she could barely run the length of the field. It was perfect, until she was dizzy all the time, and so cold she felt on the brink of freezing solid. And then all of the stuff they'd learned in health class came back in a rush, an avalanche, and Liz stopped, mostly.

Mostly.

Thanksgiving—surely that could be an exception. So much food that she couldn't help herself, and she couldn't stand feeling bloated. Christmas too, and Easter. Buffet outings. But other than that, she ate, and she kept it inside her.

That was perfect too, until one day she puked and there were little streaks of blood among the undigested food.

It was macaroni and cheese, she remembered. Little chunks of it, blood like sauce.

She was so terrified that she broke down entirely, sat against the wall and sobbed for a good half an hour, because nine hundred people died every hour from starvation, and here she was, trying to become one of them.

When the tears dried, she looked at herself in the mirror and swore she would never puke again.

Soon, though, she would go to a beach party and stare at

the sky from the top of a tower of wishes. Soon they would be buying homecoming dresses, getting their hair done, arriving at the dance, and Kennie would tell them that she was pregnant. Soon she would watch Julia double her weekly supply of ziplock bags. Soon Liz would make out with Kennie's boyfriend, go home, and make plans.

Soon she will hate what she sees in the mirror and try to change it the only way she knows how: two fingers down her throat, her dinner in the toilet.

Five days before she crashed her car, that's exactly what she did.

She tore the kitchen apart. She sat on the white couch with the TV blaring, eating chips. She drank almost an entire liter of orange soda. There was a pecan pie in the pantry that she covered with vanilla ice cream and whipped cream and attacked with a fork. There was a plate of ribs from the restaurant down the street and an entire bowl of leftover ravioli from the Italian place in downtown Meridian.

She ate and ate and tried to keep it down.

How much shit can I hold in?

It was not a rhetorical question.

The answer: *No more.*

She set aside the Styrofoam container and the pie tin and the can of whipped cream and the empty ice cream carton and the soda bottle and the bag of chips, and she got to her feet. The floor creaked as it bore her weight.

Ten minutes later, she sat on the cold tiles, her head against the bathtub, too tired to move, too tired to ever move again. She thought of that day—it seemed like so long ago, seventh grade—when she had stared at herself in the mirror and made a promise she thought she would keep.

But that was the thing. It was a different time, when she kept promises. When she thought they were meant to be kept.

She knew better now.

She dragged herself upright and walked to the mirror. She stood, she stared at the girl in the mirror with eyes that held nothing at all, and she asked, "Am I beautiful yet?"

Beautiful like Julia, who was brave enough to be different—or used to be. Beautiful like Kennie, who saw how ugly the world could be but loved it anyway. Beautiful like anyone else, beautiful like everyone else. But she wasn't, so she wanted to be so thin that everyone could see what she was like on the inside, all failing heart and shattering pieces.

No, Liz Emerson wasn't beautiful, but soon she would be dead, and it wouldn't matter anymore.

CHAPTER THIRTY-SIX

"Meridian Teen Injured in Car Crash"

*L*iam scrolls down his phone, opened to the *Meridian Daily*'s website. He scans the new article about Liz and the crash, and notices that he is mentioned in passing. "A classmate of the victim saw the crash and called the police." The article blames the crash on icy road conditions. It states that Liz was—*was*—the soccer team's captain and mentions that she scored the winning goal in the state championship last year. There are quotes about how Liz is a wonderful person, beautiful and always smiling.

Liam laughs under his breath and closes the tab. *Superficial article for a superficial girl*, but he doesn't really mean it. It irritates him that they whitewashed the truth and called Liz Emerson wonderful because she was beautiful. She would have hated it too.

Unfortunately, everyone else in the waiting room also seems to be reading that article, and after a few minutes, Liam begins to catch pieces of conversation.

"A classmate? Who was it?"

"Kennie or Julia, obviously."

"No, they didn't know until after."

"Maybe it was . . ."

". . . or . . ."

Liam pulls his hood over his head and turns his face away, and prays that the average intelligence of his classmates will not increase within the next few minutes.

"Hey, weren't the police questioning Liam yesterday?"

Damn.

"Liam? You mean the guy who plays flu—oh, hey! Liam. Liam!"

They swarm around him, and Liam has to remind himself to keep his misanthropy in check before he pushes back his hood and turns around.

"Yeah?"

"You were the one who found Liz, right? What was it like?"

It's Marcus Hills who asks. In the article, Marcus called Liz beautiful. In real life, he usually remarked upon her boobs.

I don't need to keep my misanthropy in check. It runs wild.

CHAPTER THIRTY-SEVEN

Four Days Before Liz Emerson Crashed Her Car

She woke up and decided to take a drive. She grabbed her keys and headed for the interstate, and she drove along her crash route to test the road conditions.

Dry with salt, but still icy at the edges. And it would snow between now and then, anyway, and the turn, her turn, was a tricky one even in good weather. Her accident might actually end up being an accident, and she wasn't certain if she liked the idea.

Doesn't matter, she decided. *Same result.*

The interstate rose into a low bridge, and Liz pushed down on the gas. The land sloped away, down and down and down until it melted to grass and trees.

There.

She pictured it as she drove. *Onto the bridge. Tighten grip on the wheel. Accelerate. Brake. Skid. Jerk the wheel to the right. Break through the railing. Close eyes. Fall—*

Liz grappled with the wheel as the car swerved, catching the interstate railing and leaving a streak of blue paint behind. She swallowed hard and took a breath. She had started following her own instructions.

Four more days.

She kept going, all the way to Cardinal Bay—still an unimpressive city, but it had a mall. Liz took the exit and parked. She headed for the closest store, even though the outside was too pink and expensive looking. Why not? What else did she have to do, four days before she died?

It sounded like a truth or dare question, the big cliché, the one that came late at night when everyone was tired and drunk and out of interesting questions. *What would you do with the last week of your life?*

Surely she had answered it before, or some variation. She wondered what she'd said. Travel, maybe, or skydive, or say good-bye.

She sure as hell didn't say *nothing*, but that's what she wanted to do now.

A perky bell and a perkier sales clerk greeted her the moment she stepped through the door. "Hi!" she said, and looked critically at Liz's hips. "Two? Let me show you our jeans, they're all on sale, this weekend only! Follow—"

"No," said Liz. She meant to add a *thanks* after, but it got lost on its way out of her mouth. She wandered off by herself.

It was definitely more of a Kennie store—preppy jeans and floral cardigans, lace and frills. She felt like she was interrupting a tea party, and the store was too small to really wander through. Liz liked to wander when she shopped. She liked to weave through racks, one earbud in and the other dangling by her thigh, a cup of coffee in her hand. She liked not being watched.

". . . um . . . I'm sorry. I don't mean to push the issue, but . . . I don't understand. Why didn't I—I mean, I just . . ."

Liz leaned around the dressing rooms and saw an office at the end of the hall. She pretended to examine the discarded and rejected rack, and listened.

"I'm sorry," a second voice said flatly. "The decision is final."

"I respect that," the girl said, desperate, "but I'd like to know why I didn't get the job. For future reference."

Liz leaned back again and caught a glimpse of a woman behind a desk. "Oh, dear, you just don't have the image we look for here at L'Esperance."

"What image?"

"We don't carry anything over a six, dear. We market our

clothing lines for people who are, well—*shaped* differently than you are. How would it look if one of our employees wasn't even able to fit into our shirts?"

Silence, then, and the manager added, "I'm sorry, dear. Thanks for applying, but I'm afraid you just don't belong in our store. But you'll find something, I'm sure! Best of luck."

Liz watched; the girl opened her mouth, closed it, and walked out. Her face was blotchy, and Liz wasn't sure if it was because she was angry or if it was because she was crying. Liz felt like both herself. The woman followed and caught sight of Liz.

"Hello!" she said brightly, glancing up and down Liz's body. "Are you here to apply?"

Liz looked after the girl, but she was already gone, the bell ringing cheerfully behind her. She looked at the woman and said, "Fuck you."

Back outside, holding her coat, she closed her eyes. The wind clawed her arms raw, and the snow stung where it touched her—and she remembered, suddenly, the way they used to celebrate the first snowfall. It was their very own holiday. Did the snow hurt then? She couldn't remember.

Then she got into her car, put her face in her coat, and screamed.

Had the world always been like this? Why had it seemed

so much kinder when she was younger? Why had it ever seemed beautiful?

Liz Emerson looked around and saw that laws didn't have to be followed if you could get away with breaking them. She saw that snow wasn't always beautiful. She saw that the past was a dead thing and the future held no promises, and as she leaned her forehead on the steering wheel and closed her eyes, the tears came and it really hit her that she didn't want to open her eyes ever again.

Funny things, aren't they? People. They only believed in what they could see. Appearances were all that mattered, and no one would ever care what she was like on the inside. No one cared that she was breaking apart.

As the sky grew dimmer and the streetlights came on, Liz remembered that there was a party that night, so she did the only thing she could think of. She backed out of her parking spot, bumped into the car behind her, and drove off with the other car's alarm blaring.

She drove past the turn and the hill and the tree, and she held her breath and didn't dare look. She was afraid that if she turned her head and saw it all in the falling dark, she would go, right now.

Alas, she was on the wrong side of the interstate.

Instead, she texted Julia. They were going to a party that night. Julia was going to drive. Liz was going to get drunk.

SNAPSHOT: SNOW

It is snowing.

Liz's mom is taking cookies out of the oven, and her father is setting up the record player by the fireplace. It is their own holiday, the first snowfall, a day in a snow globe, a day to turn off all the lights and pretend the world is being born.

Liz and I are outside, and this time we don't run around like Tinker Bell caught in a storm of fairy dust, we don't make wishes, we don't make snow angels. Today, the snow is white and swirling, the sky is close, and the world is so big and beautiful and infinite that we don't need to pretend. All we know is already perfect.

CHAPTER THIRTY-EIGHT

Forty-One Minutes Before Liz Emerson
Crashed Her Car

Liz spent a minute trying to remember the exact word-
ing of Newton's Second Law of Motion—something about
acceleration being directly related to the net force and
inversely proportional to the mass—so there were only
forty minutes left when she decided it didn't matter. She
knew the equation, anyway. Force equals mass times acceleration. $F = ma$.

The unit on Newton's Second Law was more math oriented
than the first or the third, so Liz had managed to get a decent
score on that test. This, however, was more of a testament
to her ability to push buttons on her calculator than any
true understanding, and forty minutes before she crashed

her car, she still didn't fully appreciate the relationship between force, mass, and acceleration.

The textbook made the world black and white and drew a very uncompromising line between what was and what could never be, as though everything was already dictated and Liz's only job was to keep breathing.

She wished they had talked more about how all of the equations were derived. She wanted to know how Galileo and Newton and Einstein discovered the things they discovered. She wanted to know how they could have lived in the exact same world as everyone else but see things that no one else did.

Forty minutes before she crashed her car, Liz began to think about Liam Oliver, who always seemed to see things that no one else did, and didn't seem to care that it was strange.

CHAPTER THIRTY-NINE
Thoughts on the Road

When Liam first saw Liz's car, he nearly crashed his own.

This was his favorite stretch of highway. Of course the only Costco was over an hour away, goddamn middle-of-nowhere Meridian—but he enjoyed the trip wholeheartedly because he was driving his mom's car and using her gas. She'd had to take his sister to piano lessons, so he'd agreed to bag his homework and run her errands. He liked these long, lonely drives. They allowed him to sort out his thoughts, and he had a lot of thoughts to sort out today.

He thought about Liz Emerson, and the party on Saturday night. She had fallen asleep against his shoulder, and he had taken her home.

There was a patch of trees on his left—he called it a forest out of pity—and a large slope on the other side, so he could see for miles. He loved this stretch because it made him feel insignificant and necessary at the same time, like everything had a reason.

Today, when he looked down the hill, he saw a Mercedes at the bottom, smoking. He thought, *That looks like Liz Emerson's car.*

He wondered briefly if he ought to call the police or something, but someone must have already, right? He had almost crossed the bridge when he did a double take; his head snapped around, and somehow, through the smoke and the distance, he caught a glimpse of green through the mangled window.

He thought, *Liz Emerson was wearing a green sweater today.*

Then he thought, *Shit.*

And then he thought nothing at all.

SNAPSHOT: ROLLING

We are rolling down an impossibly green hill. Our arms are pressed to our chests, our hair caught in our mouths, tangled with our laughter. Gravity is our playmate, momentum is our friend. We are blurs of motion. We are racing, and we are both winning, because we do not race each other.

We race the world, and as fast as it rotates, as fast as it revolves, we are faster.

CHAPTER FORTY

This Is What Liz Emerson's Car Did

*I*t rolled.

Sitting on the brown couch, she had imagined her death like this:

She veers off the road and down the hill. Her car slides, spins a few times. She hits her head and is gone. Her body is mostly whole when they find it. They'll take out her organs, and her dead body will be more useful than her living one ever was.

It did not happen like that.

About a mile before she veered, she had taken off her seat belt. She had planned to close her eyes, sit back, and let it happen. If she had paid more attention in physics, she would have known that the laws of motion are stronger than any plans she had.

On the way down, she was braced against the steering wheel, her foot jammed on the brake. Maybe if she pressed hard enough, she could stop the world from spinning.

It didn't work.

Her seat went flying forward, and her leg broke in three different places. The car landed on its roof at the bottom of the hill and slid across the icy grass into the base of the tree. She screamed and tried to find something to grab, and accidentally flung her hand out the broken window, where the car briefly pinned it against the ground and shattered it. The car slammed into the tree, flattening the passenger side, and the force shoved Liz's head outside.

Then everything stilled, and she laid in the nest of glass and stared at the sky.

CHAPTER FORTY-ONE

Gravity

*L*iam was aware, for once, that there was a party going on that night. It was at Joshua Willis's house, and (since Joshua was the head senior stoner) it was going to be near the upper end of the wildness gradient.

The only reason he knew was because he lived a block away. Gossip reached Liam slowly; usually by the time he heard about parties, they were over. But on that night, in the quiet darkness of his bedroom, he was close enough to hear the screams and laughter.

Staring at the invisible ceiling, he wondered what it was like at these parties. He wondered what it was like to get drunk and not care.

That night, not for the first time, he yearned to be a part of it.

Normally, Liam was quite content to be a misfit. He did not particularly care that he sat in the outer ring of the cafeteria during lunch. He was not concerned with what people said about him. A lot of bullying was indirect and a lot of bullies didn't know they were bullies, and maybe some of them didn't even mean to be—he could see this quite clearly, and it no longer bothered him. He knew who he was.

There was a certain freedom in being on the outside. He watched instead of being watched. After Liz had shredded his reputation during freshman year, Liam surrendered to things he had earlier resisted for the sake of appearance. He read Thoreau in public, stopped spending money on uncomfortable clothes, took down his posters of bikini-clad models and covered his walls with song lyrics and quotes. He embraced his weirdness, and it was nice.

But sometimes—tonight—he wanted more.

The noise kept him awake until about two in the morning, when someone finally called the police and the party dispersed, and in the silence left behind, Liam heard someone puking.

He tried to ignore it, but—God, those were some awful retching noises. He sighed and got out of bed and pulled his curtains aside to see a figure walking unsteadily through the park, which was really more of an overgrown field with a tetanus-ridden playground, by his house. Dammit. He had to be a good person now, didn't he? He put on a jacket and went out to investigate.

He found Liz Emerson lying on the wood chips, shivering.

Liam just stared at her for a moment, wondering what the hell he had done to deserve this, a very drunk girl whom he'd had a crush on since fifth grade, half asleep and all alone beside his house.

Almost alone, he thought, and crouched down beside her.

Liz Emerson was generally a pretty person, but with her eyes bloodshot and dribbles of vomit still hanging on her chin, she was decidedly not tonight. She was not pretty, but there was something beautiful about her all the same.

"Damn it," he said under his breath. "Damn it all. Liz?"

"Jake?" she asked groggily, and tried to kiss him.

Liam had spent many hours devoted to fantasies of kissing Liz Emerson, but in none of them had she smelled of puke and alcohol, and in none of them had she believed that he was Jake Derrick, so he declined. He propped her upright and held her by the shoulders when it became evident that she could not sit on her own.

"Liz," he said. "Did you drive?"

"No, silly," she mumbled. "Julia."

"Damn it," Liam muttered, looking closer at her eyes. "You're not high too, are you? God. You are."

Liz laughed muddily and tried to get to her feet. "Julia went home 'cause she's too goody and stuff, an' I told her Kennie'd take me home . . . but Kennie and Kyle are swallowing each other . . . so I'll walk . . . s'all right . . ."

"Right," said Liam, and pulled her up. "Okay. I'm going to drive you home."

She made no reply, only leaned into his shoulder and passed out.

"Damn it," Liam said again.

He walked a few steps like that, dragging Liz behind him, and then he gave in and picked her up. *I am holding Liz Emerson,* Liam thought, and then he thought it again because he couldn't quite believe it. *Liz Emerson is in my arms.*

She was warm, and smaller than he'd thought she'd be.

He put her in the front seat of his beat-up LeBaron and briefly considered going inside to tell his mom about his late-night trip across town, but decided against it. She wouldn't wake up, and he didn't know how to explain, anyway.

"You . . . kidnapping me?" Liz mumbled as Liam backed out of his driveway.

"Depends," he replied. "Are you going to puke in my car?"

She did.

"Damn it."

They drove the rest of the way in silence. Liam knew where Liz lived—everyone knew where Liz lived. This, however, was the first time he had ever seen her house up close, and he didn't know why the idea of going inside made him so uncomfortable.

He cleared his throat and said, "Liz, do you have your keys?"

She didn't answer. Liam turned off the car and asked again in the silence, and then twice more before she finally slurred, "Doooormat."

Liam got out of the car, and then went to the passenger side and dragged her out behind him. He climbed the steps with Liz limp in his arms and crouched awkwardly with her propped against his shoulder, and rummaged around until he found the key taped to the underside of the welcome mat.

"That," he said, "is depressingly stupid."

He heaved both of them up and unlocked the door, and fumbled for a light switch. Inside, the house was just as big as it had looked on the outside; beautiful, he supposed, all clean lines and sharp edges, but lonely, somehow. As he walked through the foyer, it struck him that perhaps the idiotic placement of the spare key was not the most depressing thing about this house, after all.

He tried to lower Liz onto a white couch in the living room but ended up kind of dropping her—he was tired, and Liam was not exactly well-off in terms of upper body strength. Then he stood there and looked around, and when he looked back, Liz was untouchable again. This was where she belonged, and he did not.

So he left.

He was only halfway through the foyer when he heard her.

"Liam," she sighed. "Thanks."

He hesitated. He almost turned around, stayed with her.

Instead, he kept walking, through the high-ceilinged foyer and out the door. He turned off the lights before he stepped into the cold and left her to sleep in darkness.

Liam told himself that Liz would be too drunk to remember. On Monday, when she gave no more acknowledgment of his existence than she ever had, he figured that he was right.

He wasn't.

When Liz woke up, she ran to the bathroom and puked. After, she leaned against the toilet and put her head against the wall, and she thought of him. She wondered. Why.

She was tired. Gravity pulled at her more aggressively than usual. When she closed her eyes, she could feel it, dragging her deeper, deeper.

I would have pulled her back. I would have saved her from falling, but she didn't see my hand.

CHAPTER FORTY-TWO

Thirty-Eight Minutes Before Liz Emerson Crashed Her Car

*G*ravity.

That was the ultimate force, wasn't it? The last acceleration. And then the crash.

Maybe, she thought, *he sees something that no one else can see. In me.*

And then she laughed.

She didn't really understand gravity, but then she didn't really understand Liam either. She drove and remembered his eyes in the light of the ridiculous chandelier, the odd grace of his fingers, the way he called her stupid without scorn.

They were very hazy, the memories, and she supposed

that was her own fault. Alcohol and pot—she didn't remember much of that night, but she remembered Liam.

It was ironic because she had other, clearer memories of Liam that she would much, much rather forget, and never would.

But she supposed that was her fault too.

CHAPTER FORTY-THREE
Glances

*J*ulia and Kennie sit with Liz's mom. Both of them watch Liam, and both of them are trying to keep the other from noticing.

"I hope my mom doesn't come back," Kennie says quickly to Julia, when Julia catches her glancing around the waiting room again.

"She won't," says Julia. "Doesn't she have a church meeting or something? I'll take you home. I don't know where my keys are, though." She looks across the room, though her keys are in her pocket.

And so it goes.

Julia is tempted to go over and finally apologize for what

they did, but why should Liam listen to her? Kennie, on the other hand, remembers all the horrible things she's said about him and starts crying again, because she doesn't remember exactly when she turned into such an awful human being.

Liam stares out the window.

CHAPTER FORTY-FOUR

Thirty-Five Minutes Before Liz Emerson Crashed Her Car

*T*hey had acceleration, she, Kennie, and Julia. They had mass. They goaded and mocked and multiplied each other, and so they had force. They were the catalysts, the fingers that tipped the first domino. They started things that grew into other things that were much greater than themselves.

A touch, a nudge in the wrong direction, and everyone fell down.

CHAPTER FORTY-FIVE
Falling

On the first day of fifth grade, Liz was sitting on the swing beside Liam's at recess, falling and flying. Her hair fanned out behind her and her eyes were closed, and that was what had caught his attention, her closed eyes. She looked a little bit silly and very much alive, and Liam couldn't stop watching.

Liz, on her part, was aware that the boy beside her was watching, but she loved swinging too much to care what he thought. She loved the wind hitting her face and the brief moment of suspension at the top of the arc and the falling sensation that was magnified by the darkness of her eyelids. She imagined that she was a bird, an angel, a wayward star.

At the height of the arc, she let go. And she flew.

Liam watched with his mouth hanging wide open, expecting her to crumple on the asphalt and die tragically before his eyes.

She didn't, and when she walked away, Liam's heart followed.

The year after, they started middle school and chose electives for the first time. Liz and Julia chose choir. Kennie and Liam chose band, which was fine, but they both chose to play the flute, which was not.

Liam became the first boy in the history of Meridian to sit in the flute section, and he didn't mind because he was damn good.

Kennie did mind, because Liam was *damn good*, better than she would ever be, which meant that she would be stuck in second chair for the rest of her life.

On the second day of freshman year, Kennie stomped out of band fuming about how Liam was a kiss-ass and a dick and totally full of himself, and Liz, tired of her crap, interrupted to say, "Then do something about it."

Kennie stopped short. "What?"

Liz shrugged. "You always complain, but you never do anything about it. So let's do something about it."

The plan fell into place very quickly after that.

CHAPTER FORTY-SIX

The Ruining of Liam Oliver

*T*here were three phases.

Phase one took place during lunch on the first day of their freshman homecoming week. The inner ring was empty, because they were all standing in the hallway, waiting to vote for the homecoming court. The outer ring stayed put. What was the point? Everyone knew Liz Emerson would win, and probably Jimmy Travis. Whatever. *Too much trouble, making crowns and shit,* they told themselves. The only way any of them would ever make it onto court would be if Liz Emerson herself made it happen.

For freshman homecoming, that was exactly what she did.

She told everyone to vote for Liam Oliver, the only boy to play the flute. The guys laughed and threw the word *gay* around, and the girls shrugged because they couldn't care less which boy was voted onto court.

Liam was in band, fingering through "Fate of the Gods," when Dylan Madlen, the senior class president, came on the intercom to announce the court, and Liam nearly dropped his flute when he heard his name follow Liz Emerson's.

For a wild moment, he thought that this was the beginning of something—maybe the money he'd spent on new clothes hadn't been a waste. But then he looked around and everyone was sniggering, and reality set in.

Well.

What an exquisite joke.

He stared at his flute, at his warped reflection, and he didn't look up again until the bell rang.

They executed phase two the next day, during sixth hour. Liz had a fake pass to the guidance office, and she used it to get out of geometry. Kennie left Spanish to go to the bathroom and met her under the stairs. Julia took a little longer—it had taken some convincing to get her out of honors biology at all—but eventually she showed up, and together they headed for the band room.

"Idiot," Liz said to Kennie as they walked through the

deserted hallways. They looked ridiculous—that day's homecoming theme was the eighties, and they were all in neon leggings and oversized windbreakers. "How the hell are you going to explain why you were in the bathroom for half an hour?"

Kennie frowned. Her face was barely visible under all her teased hair. "Digestion troubles?"

"Feminine needs," Julia suggested. "Say you had to go find a tampon or something. Jacobsen's afraid of women."

"Ooooh," said Kennie, perking up. "Can I borrow a tampon?"

"You don't actually need one, stupid," said Liz, stopping in front of the band-room door. "Now shut up. Let's go."

Liam had study hall this hour, and more often than not, he used it to practice his flute. Liz, who had never played an instrument in her life, found it difficult to believe that he was actually practicing. And since he wasn't practicing, he was definitely doing something else—hopefully something monumentally and hilariously embarrassing. She was going to catch him at it.

"Come on," she said unnecessarily to Julia and Kennie, and they snuck inside.

The practice rooms were along one wall of the band room, and in the far one, someone was playing.

They peeked through the narrow window.

Liam's back was to them. He was playing his flute.

They waited five, ten, fifteen minutes.

Liam kept playing his flute.

"This is stupid," Liz finally whispered.

Except she didn't really mean it. She wasn't bored. She listened to Liam play and was mesmerized, because it was so obvious that he was happy. It made her remember that there had once been a time when she was in love with the sunshine and the wind and each brief flight.

It was like watching the sky change colors, his playing.

And then it made her jealous, because Liz Emerson was never at peace like that. Not really. Not anymore.

Very suddenly, Liam stopped. They dropped to their stomachs with their breaths sucked in—but Liam hadn't seen them. He was just fixing the music stand, or he was trying to.

"Damn it," Liz heard Liam mutter. "Just . . . pull . . . out . . ."

Kennie stifled a snort against Liz's shoulder. "That's what she said," she giggled.

And there it was.

The brilliantly, monumentally, hilariously embarrassing moment.

Liz pulled her phone out of her pocket so quickly that she nearly elbowed Kennie in the face. She pulled up her camera app, angled the lens at the crack beneath the door, and pressed the record button.

"And here," she whispered, "we see Liam Oliver in his natural habitat, enjoying the primary pastime of his species: *playing* with his flute."

Liam walked past, the bottom of his jeans worn, his Converses on the brink of falling apart. That was all they could see, really, but that was all they needed. There was some banging, and Kennie giggled again.

"Come on," came his muffled voice. "A little higher, damn it."

And then he actually grunted, and not even Julia could keep from laughing. The camera shook as they pressed their faces in one another's shoulders, trying to keep quiet.

There was a dull crash—Liam had lost his balance and fallen against the wall, but it didn't look that way on camera. Kennie gave a half giggle, half hiccup, and on the other side of the door, Liam froze.

But by the time he looked out the window, they were gone.

Liz sent the video to her entire list of contacts. By the end of the day, it seemed like everyone had seen it. Someone had put it on Facebook, and someone else had uploaded it to YouTube. At her locker after the final bell, she saw people laugh when Liam walked by in the hallway, and Liz turned away, because it made her feel weird, somewhere deep, when she saw his bewildered face.

Still, she went home and prepared for phase three.

Liam Oliver is a pervert.

Liam Oliver is gay.

Liam Oliver is in a threesome.

Liam Oliver gets turned on by inanimate objects.

Liam Oliver chewed on the lead paint of his crib as a child and is therefore permanently fucked up.

Liam Oliver will screw anything.

Those were the more appropriate rumors.

Phase three should have been an easy victory. Of course, everyone said that the football game would be too, and by the end of the first quarter, they were down 14-0. All of Meridian was packed onto the bleachers, soaking wet and screaming. The air smelled like rain and fish—the booster club always held a fish fry before the homecoming game, and tonight the sky was made of scales and oil and losing.

Liz stood on the rickety bleachers, stomping and jumping and screaming, dressed in nothing but a sports bra and shorts and paint. To her right, Julia was the only one in the student section who was sitting, her arms crossed tightly over her chest because the rain was making her bra half-transparent. To her left, Kennie was gripping Liz's arm with all her strength, because Jenna Erikson had fallen off the bleachers earlier and broken her leg. Kennie pressed herself into Liz's side and whined that the rain would wash Riley Striver's name off her stomach before he could see it. Liz didn't care. The JAKE DERRICK on her stomach had long since turned to watercolor.

But it was worse when the rain finally stopped. The fog was thick and it trapped the lights, and at halftime, after the band show ended, Liz shook Kennie off and made her way down the bleachers with the rest of the homecoming court, shoebox in hand. She held it carefully—Liam's crown was inside.

The freshman girls cheered for her as she crossed the track to the field. Liz could hear Kennie's scream above them all.

The boys were yelling too, but not for her, and they weren't cheering.

Liam was behind her. His falling-apart Converses squished in the mud, steps echoing hers. And suddenly that was all that mattered—her feet and his feet and the distance between them. It was like a dance, and the music was made of the screams of their classmates: step, *gay*, step, *pervert*, step, *faggot*. It hurt her ears.

She wanted to turn around. She wanted to take his hand and pull him . . . where? Where would she have led him?

She glanced over her shoulder, and he looked away.

They reached the center of the field and took their places in line with the other court members. At the front of the court lineup, Kate Dulmes laughed when she saw Liam and nudged Brandon Jason, and Brandon made an obscene hand gesture while the principal dug through his pockets for the list of their names.

"Hey, Liam," Brianna Vern, one of the sophomore representatives, said, leaning out of the lineup to smile at him. "Nice of you guys to join us. We were just talking about how much easier it is to be a boy than a girl. Like, you guys don't have periods or anything. And, I mean, you *love* your body parts."

"Dude, she's right," said Matthew Derringer. He was the other sophomore representative, and one of Jake's best friends. Liz wasn't sure why, but she always had to fight down the urge to hug him when he was near. Lean in and wrap her arms around him and knee him in his unsuspecting balls. Hard. "I do love my body parts. I reward 'em. What about you, Liam? When was the last time you rewarded that flute of yours? Just now, on the bleachers? Thought I could feel them shaking."

The fog. How it magnified.

The laughter. The screaming—*gay pervert faggot gaypervertfaggot.* The digging, Liz's fingernails against palms, teeth, and lips. And the silence. Heavy heavy heavy silence.

Somewhere in the fog, the principal announced Kate and Mike as king and queen.

The crown Kate had made for Mike was heavy and elaborate and beautiful, and his for her was from Burger King. There was a pause and furious clicking as the parents took pictures. Someone complained that they should move the crowning back to the dance, when everyone was dressed up, though no one listened. The names continued. Junior representatives, sophomore.

Liz's eyes flickered to Liam.

She wondered if he had watched the video—watched it all the way through.

"Your freshman representatives: Liz Emerson and Liam Oliver!"

Liz drew her crown from the shoebox. She had gone online and bought the cheapest, crappiest flute she could find. Jake had cut it to pieces in his metals class, and she had hot-glued it back together in a rough circle, and now she pulled it from its nest of tissue paper and offered it to Liam.

His face.

Why did you come? She wanted to scream it. *Why the hell*

did you come? Idiot, you goddamn idiot. You knew this would happen. You knew what we would do. What I would do.

You deserve this, she tried to think, but couldn't. *You brought this upon yourself.*

There was a lump in her throat, and she wasn't sure why.

He stared at the crown for a long time. He stared while fuzzy cheerleader shapes unfurled a big paper sign: MERIDIAN HOMECOMING, GO FIGHT WIN! He stared while Nick Braden tripped while running back onto the field and the rest of the team went down on top of him. He stared while the crowd booed. He stared while the football coach finally lost his temper and began to scream at the court to "Get your asses off the field!" and the team to "Get your asses together!"

It was killing her, his silence. She took a breath to break it wide open, and then he finally looked up.

Here Liz was supposed to say something, something horrible, and smile to show all of her teeth, but the only word she could remember was his name. She tried to say it. She couldn't.

After a moment, he took the crown from her hands, dropped his own shoebox at her feet, and walked off the field.

Liz stared after him, her throat closed and her eyes strangely full, and then she looked down. The lid had fallen aside when the box hit the ground, and she could see the tip of a crown.

It was beautiful, and suddenly, she knew. That's why he came. To give her the crown.

The mud splattered her knees as she dropped down beside the shoebox—it was cold, and the coldness spread. She reached for the crown, pushed the tissue paper aside. Wire and gold leaf and metallic spray paint, twisted and braided and looped. It looked impossible, and she touched the edges to make sure it wasn't.

She spun around. "Liam!"

There was no answer.

"You," the football coach roared, marching toward her. "You have three seconds to get your ass off the field, or I will *carry it off.*"

Later, Meridian would lose the game 49-2, and Liz Emerson would slip away from Kennie and Julia to run all around the football field in search of Liam to say . . . something. She didn't know. Anything. Everything.

But while she was pushing people away and peeling them apart, she saw a ziplock bag sticking out of a stranger's pocket, and she took it because she was too tired to keep looking.

CHAPTER FORTY-SEVEN
The Effects

*L*iam didn't go to the dance, but it didn't matter.

Surely it was okay to laugh. It was funny. A nerd had been voted onto court and had gotten caught . . . practicing. And besides, no one really got hurt. Liz, Kennie, and Julia went to the dance and grinded on the sweat-slippery floor, and then they went to parties and got drunk and forgot all about it.

On Monday, Liam quit band.

When the teacher tried to change his mind, he threw his flute against the wall and walked away.

△ ▽ △

Many people guessed that Liam cried when he watched the video.

They were wrong.

Liam watched with no emotion whatsoever.

No one guessed that Liz cried when she watched it.

After Liam quit band and left his dented and ruined flute behind, she watched the video again and again. She deleted it and cried because she couldn't do anything. She couldn't drag the video back from all the people she had sent it to, or all the people they had sent it to. She couldn't take it off the internet. She couldn't put Liam's flute back together. So she didn't try.

CHAPTER FORTY-EIGHT

Thirty-Three Minutes Before Liz Emerson
Crashed Her Car

Liz thought about Liam Oliver in terms of Newton's Second Law of Motion.

Mass. Liz managed to gather an enormous audience. The video spread like a virus. Towns an hour away knew about Liam Oliver. Kids would stop him at Walmart and ask, smirking, about his flute.

Acceleration. There was no unit that could accurately measure the speed, the potential and kinetic energy, of gossip. It made sound look like a tortoise. It made light look like Kennie's crippled grandma. There was a strange addiction in the act of spreading a rumor, relishing someone else's pain. No one could resist.

Force. Liz. She looked around and saw all of the broken things in her wake, and then she looked inside herself and saw the spidering cracks from the weight of all the things she had done. She hated what she was and didn't know how to change, and half an hour before she drove her car off the road, she saw that despite all of that, she didn't have enough force to stop the world from turning.

But she had enough to stop her own.

After Liam, there were others.

There was Lauren Melbrook, who began dating Lucas Drake after he dumped Kennie. They were a cute couple and they made Kennie cry. So one morning that January, Liz, Julia, and Kennie woke up early to spray-paint SLUT across the snow on Lauren's front lawn. They took pictures, uploaded them to Facebook, and tagged Lauren in all of them. Lucas Drake dumped her on the very same day.

There was Sandra Garrison, who told Mrs. Schumacher, their Algebra II teacher, that Liz had copied off her test. Mrs. Schumacher believed her, but Sandra had no proof, so Mrs. Schumacher let it go, but Liz (because she had, in fact, cheated on the test) felt it necessary to spread a rumor that Sandra Garrison was pregnant. Being a stress eater, Sandra did indeed gain weight after the rumors made their rounds. Liz later spread a follow-up rumor that Sandra had aborted her baby, which marked the death of her already nose-diving social status.

There was Justin Strayes, who had made fun of Julia's strained relationship with her father. Liz planted a small bag of pot in his locker on a day the drug dogs came. There was an enormous investigation, and Justin ended up missing quite a bit of school to appear in court. When he came back, no one would look him in the eye. It was okay to experiment. It was not okay to get caught. Justin had gotten caught, and now no one talked to him except the stoners.

They all became numbers in Liz's metaphorical body count.

CHAPTER FORTY-NINE

Twenty-Nine Minutes Before Liz Emerson Crashed Her Car

*L*iz wondered why Lauren Melbrook had never spray-painted HYPOCRITE across her lawn.

CHAPTER FIFTY
What Liz Didn't Know

*L*iam never actually quit playing the flute.

He quit band. But band had always been stupid. He smashed his flute. But he had three others at home.

There were days on which he was tempted to give up entirely. He never seriously considered suicide—in fact, he wasn't quite sure how to do it; was dropping a toaster into your bathtub still a thing?—but it passed through his mind a few times.

What the video really did was this: it made him see why so many people hated Liz Emerson, and he also saw why they all followed her. Liz Emerson got drunk too easily, and on just about anything: alcohol, power, expectations.

She was never careful with her life or anyone else's, and in her disregard was a coldness, a deep cruelty, a willingness to destroy anyone, everyone.

He went on. He played his flute. He found that there were still beautiful things in the world, and nothing could ever change that.

And one day, he decided to forgive Liz Emerson.

It was near the beginning of sophomore year. It had been cloudy on and off that day. Liam had stayed after school to finish editing his piece for the literary magazine, and when he left the building, he realized that he was not alone.

Liz Emerson was waiting for a ride. Judging by the small ring of sweat on her T-shirt and the state of her hair, she had just finished cross-country practice. They ignored each other studiously. Liam stood in the shadows of the building, and Liz stood in the dull and uncertain light, her head bent over her phone, her shoulder pushed against the brickwork.

Liam watched her in silence and remembered how he had felt when he first saw the video, and he never wanted to punch anyone as much as he wanted to punch Liz Emerson then.

He saw it in his head: him, crossing the distance between them, his ratty Converses scraping against the gum-dotted cement; her, turning in surprise and then away again in disgust, his curled fist—

Then he laughed to himself, because everyone knew that Liz Emerson could punch harder than he could.

He was about to turn away when suddenly the clouds moved apart and a sliver of sky peeked through. When he looked again at Liz, her head was thrown back and she was staring at that slice of blue with her eyes wide.

Then the clouds shifted and the blue was gone, and for a second, Liz's face was so vulnerable and indignant that Liam almost expected her to fight her way up and push the clouds apart with her fingers.

The gritting of tires against asphalt made Liam straighten and glance away, and when he looked back, Liz was getting into a car.

As she drove off, he forgave her because he realized that Liz Emerson yearned for beautiful things too.

SNAPSHOT: ABOVE

It is her sixth birthday, and her father has made all of her wishes come true.

Her nose is pressed against the small, round airplane window. Outside, the clouds are mountains upon waves, curving in great spirals that make her dizzy when she tries to follow them. Everywhere, everywhere is the sun and the sky, and the entire world is below her.

When she comes home that night, Monica will ask her how the airplane ride was, and she'll talk for hours about all that she saw. Then she'll come to me and describe it all again, but she'll be far away. I was very familiar with the way Liz's eyes lit up when she spoke of flying, but I will not see the gleam.

She takes my hands and I hold hers tightly, because I already know what she'll realize very soon: she is human and bound by the same laws of nature—gravity, in particular—as everyone else.

Try as she might, she will never grow wings.

CHAPTER FIFTY-ONE

Three Days Before Liz Emerson Crashed Her Car

*L*iz had not wanted company that day. She was nursing a massive, massive hangover, and her mouth still tasted like puke. She hadn't finished her physics project—she was trying, but she was still so vastly confused about Liam that she couldn't concentrate. The fact that Jake was here pissed her off, because they both knew that the only reason he was here was because her TV was bigger than his and she had surround sound, so the noise of his machine gun on Call of Duty was "fucking awesome." Liz was sitting on the couch with her physics binder spilling across the cushions and writing GRAVITY IS GRAVITY IS ALWAYS GRAVITY over and over again, and Jake was telling her to put it in terms of derivatives in between curses at the screen—and all of a sudden she was just very tired of him, so she put down her pencil and finally accused him of cheating on her.

She had known about it since almost the beginning. Hell, the first time he kissed her, he was still dating Hannah Carstens.

Three weeks after they had started dating, she, Julia, and Kennie were walking across the parking lot to Kennie's brother's car. They came around the corner of the school and fell silent, because right in front of them, Jake Derrick was making out with a girl who was decidedly not Liz Emerson.

Julia and Kennie both spun around to look at Liz, and Liz had honestly been too stunned to be hurt. She had stared for a moment, and then she turned on her heel and walked away, with Julia and Kennie close behind.

That night, she texted Jake.

Hey. It's not working. We're done, okay? Bye.

Over the weekend, he texted her sixty-seven times, going back and forth between *what the fuck did I do?* and *Liz, I'm so sorry, please give me a second chance, I won't do it again. I'm so sorry, babe* and *why the hell won't you just text me back?*

She didn't respond.

They stayed broken up for exactly one week. The next Friday, Liz was walking through the hall with Kennie when Jake caught her wrist, spun her around, and kissed her.

"Liz," he whispered against her lips. His fingers were tangled in her hair and on her waist, his forehead brushing hers. He was everywhere. "Liz, I'm sorry, okay? I am. Listen to me—god, Liz. Just don't tell me it's over."

With the entire hallway watching and Kennie going "Awwww!" behind her, Liz couldn't.

She knew that Jake didn't mean anything he said. He didn't even know what he was supposedly sorry for. She knew that he was still hoping that she hadn't found out about him and whichever girl it had been that time— Sarah Hannigan?

Still, she convinced herself that he wouldn't do it again.

She was wrong, of course.

Jake cheated on her again, and again, and again. He did it so often that he convinced himself that Liz was too stupid and too in love with him to notice—besides, the others were just flings, just for fun. Liz was the one who mattered to him. Or at least, he wanted it to look that way.

But on that day, three days before she drove her car into a tree, in the middle of a quickly intensifying argument, Liz simply did not want to deal with him anymore.

"What the f— ? No, *damn it*!" Jake almost fell over as he tried to shoot a terrorist on the screen. He glanced around at where she lay sprawled across the white couch. "What the fuck is your problem? Why are you just bitching at everything I say?"

Get out of my house. That's what Liz wanted to say. *Get out and don't come back.* Instead she said, "I don't know, Jake. Why don't you ask Natalie Zimmer?"

She watched Jake's hands tense on the controller, but he didn't look away from the screen. "What the hell are you talking about?"

Liz exploded. She knew about everything. She knew about Sammie Graham, with whom he had sexted all through sophomore year. She knew about Abby Carey, who had aborted a baby over the summer that she had not made with her boyfriend. She knew about Bailey Henry, who had been responsible for the hickey on his neck when he came back from the bathroom during their last homecoming.

She watched Jake go pale and then red, and before she could finish, he threw down the controller and snarled in her face. "Don't pretend like you're so innocent, Liz. You don't think I know about you and Kyle on New Year's? Yeah," he sneered when she was momentarily speechless, "that's right. He told me. What about you? Did you tell Kennie that you fucked her boyfriend?"

For the record, Liz had not slept with Kennie's boyfriend. She'd made out with him. She had been drunk and lonely and breaking into a thousand pieces, and she had needed someone to hold her together.

"You're such a slut, Liz," said Jake. "You walk around with your nose in the air like you're so much fucking better than everyone else, but you know what? You're not."

It was the way he said it. Liz never thought she was better than anyone. She thought she was so much worse that in three days, she would drive her car off the road because she didn't think that she deserved to share a planet with seven billion people who were immeasurably better than she was.

It was the way he laughed.

After he left, Liz sat back down on the white couch and wondered if there was such a thing as love. She couldn't remember much of her parents' relationship—from what she remembered, they had been happy. Her entire childhood had been happy. Back then, she'd thought that the world was a wonderful place, and look how wrong she had turned out to be.

She thought of Kennie's parents, and Julia's, and how none of them were happy.

Liz believed love was unconditional, and the longer she sat on the couch and stared at the screen, where Jake's avatar was filling with bullets, the less convinced she was about the existence of love.

Still, she had to make sure. And since her theory didn't apply solely to romantic love, she called her mother.

The phone rang twelve times. Liz was about to hang up when her mother finally picked up.

"Liz?" Her mother's voice was frazzled and far away. "What is it?"

"Mom?" Liz had to clear her throat because her voice was so small. "Mom, I . . ."

She didn't know what to say. *Do you love me?* Even in her head, it sounded stupid.

Monica let the silence last for about five seconds. "Liz, can this wait? I thought this was an emergency. You know this is an international call, right? I'm in Rio right now, remember?"

"Yeah, I remember, Mom. I just—"

"Honey, I had to leave the meeting to answer this. I can barely understand what the man is saying as it is—his accent is so heavy. What do you need?"

What did she need? Liz Emerson knew what she needed. What she truly needed was help, but she didn't know the words to ask for it.

"Mom," Liz finally whispered. "I think I'm sick."

"Oh, well, there's some Tylenol in the pantry. You know that. I have to go, okay, Liz? I'll be back Wednesday—" Her mother paused and cleared her throat.

Of course she was coming back on Wednesday. Monica had missed New Year's and Easter and Halloween and the first snowfall, but she would never miss the anniversary of her husband's death.

"Wednesday. Stay warm. Drink some soup. Okay, I really need to go." Monica hesitated, and her voice was distant when she said, "Love you, sweetie. Bye."

CALL ENDED.

Liz stared at the screen. Her mother's words echoed through her head: *love you.* People threw them around so easily, as if they were nothing, as if they meant nothing.

She stood and popped Jake's game out of the Xbox, cracked it in half, and went to clean her room. Liz didn't want to leave any clues behind, and if anyone saw the state of her room, the accident story would be considerably less believable.

CHAPTER FIFTY-TWO

Hopes and Fears

*L*iz's mother has noticed Liam.

She had been wondering where Liz's boyfriend was when she remembered the boy who had been sitting near the window since yesterday afternoon. She doesn't know that Liam was the one who called the police, or what he has to do with Liz, or even his name. She only knows that he has been sitting in the same place for a very long time.

So she buys him a cup of coffee.

Liam has his hood pulled down over his head, and his eyes are closed. Monica wonders briefly if he and Liz are dating, which would explain why Jake Derrick has not come, and why this boy has been here all night and all day.

He's a nice-looking boy, very different from the other boys that Liz has brought home over the years, and she hopes that this one stays.

Monica sets down the coffee and begins to walk away, but Liam's quiet "Thank you" makes her stop, turn, and look at him again. A lump rises in her throat as he watches her; she can see clearly that he wants to ask for news but is too afraid of the answer. So Monica tries to smile and fails utterly, and then she walks away, leaving Liam with a crappy cup of coffee.

CHAPTER FIFTY-THREE

Tact, or Lack Thereof

While Liam sips his coffee, a group of Liz's less-than-friends, more-than-acquaintances plays cards on the other side of the waiting room.

"Jacobsen was such an ass about it," one of them says. "Dude, he gave us homework. Yeah, like I'm going to do homework tonight. Liz is dying, and he expects us to memorize all of the irregulars in the preterit tense?"

"Yeah, Macmillan still made us take our test in AP Physics. 'It's a college course' and all that shit," says someone, laying down a nine of clubs.

Across the table, someone sighs. "Damn it. I fold."

"And then," Nine of Clubs continues, "she started talking

about the physics of car crashes. Like, what the hell? Ever heard of fucking tact?"

He says it rather loudly. The few people who sit waiting for someone other than Liz Emerson look tempted to ask him the same question.

"Eliezer didn't make us do anything." His name is Thomas Bane, and he and Liz had a brief fling earlier this year while she was on a break from Jake. "I think the guy was crying in the back room."

"Or he was with Mr. Stephens. Doing something else in the back room."

This, however, apparently crosses a line. Every head turns to glare at the speaker, and Thomas Bane says, "Dude. Not the time."

They fall silent, staring at the cards. For a moment, I wonder if Liz was wrong. Maybe people really are less selfish in the face of pain.

Then someone else sighs.

"Damn," he says. "I fold too."

CHAPTER FIFTY-FOUR

Twenty-Four Minutes Before Liz Emerson Crashed Her Car

She remembered the Emily Dickinson poem stenciled on the wall of the English room. She could see it as she drove, black words against a yellowing wall:

> *If I can stop one heart from breaking,*
> *I shall not live in vain;*
> *If I can ease one life the aching,*
> *Or cool one pain,*
> *Or help one fainting robin*
> *Unto his nest again,*
> *I shall not live in vain.*

But she had, hadn't she? She had lived in vain.

△ ▽ △

Second semester of sophomore year had just started. All of the winter teams were beginning to prepare for state tournaments, and spring athletes were getting in shape for their seasons. Julia had a dentist appointment that day, and when Liz finished her weight training, Kennie was still in dance practice. Liz stood alone in the gym lobby, scrolling through her messages, trying to tune out the echoing hoots of the basketball team as they finished their drills.

When she looked up again, half the boys had left, and the other half were huddled in a corner, laughing.

Liz heard the word *queer* and walked toward them. When she got closer, she realized that the solid mass of boy was not, in fact, a solid mass, but a number of sweaty, tall, laughing assholes surrounding Veronica Strauss.

Liz heard footsteps behind her and turned to see Kennie coming down the stairs with her jazz shoes in one hand. She was singing in a cheerfully off-key voice, beaming at Liz as she skipped across the gym lobby to join her. She stopped abruptly when she caught sight of the basketball boys.

"Hey," she said. Kennie had a habit of drawing out her *heys* in an annoying fashion that Liz had had to adapt to or go insane, but this time it was quieter and confused. She too had caught sight of Veronica Strauss behind the polyester basketball shorts.

Liz looked around for the coach. He was cleaning his

whistle on his shirt with his back to his team. Liz was almost certain that he was not deaf, but he was faithfully playing the part.

It was when the guys began touching Veronica that Liz finally thought *no.*

"Come on," Zack Hayes was saying. His right arm was braced on the wall above Veronica's head, and his face was inches from hers. She was wincing, either from his breath or his lack of deodorant or fear; Liz suspected it was a mix of all three. "Babe, you can't know what you want if you haven't tried, right? How do you know that you don't like dick, huh?" He moved closer and put his other hand on the small of her back. "I mean, if you ever want to try . . . just ask."

The basketball players were falling over themselves with laughter, but Liz, frankly, couldn't see what was funny. She hadn't gone to church since her father died, but Liz very clearly remembered a kind, gray-haired Sunday school teacher telling that everyone was different, and she should try very hard to love them all.

She had failed at that, of course.

The boys had begun to notice Liz, and they parted enough to let her through. She elbowed a number of them in their stomachs, and didn't apologize.

"Zack," she said. "Get your shitty BO out of her face."

Zack started, turned, and then relaxed again when he

saw her. "Hey, Liz," he said easily. "What's up?"

"What the hell?" said Liz.

"Oh." Zack grinned. "We're just trying to, you know, convince Veronica here. I mean, it isn't like you aren't hot or anything," he added in Veronica's direction. "I'm sure a ton of guys would sleep with you if you'd let them."

"Zack," Liz said. "Don't be an asshole."

"What?" Zack moved away from Veronica and turned to face Liz. "Come on, Liz. You know it's not natural. I mean, she's probably just confused. Like, if—"

"Raping her won't convince her," Liz said.

Zack stopped short, and the rest of the team fell silent. Liz held his gaze and dared him to say something. It was the first time she had ever said anything about the party, that party, and part of her wished that he would take the bait. She wanted to punch him. She knew how many girls Zack had slept with, and she knew how many of them hadn't wanted him there. He knew. His friends knew. The basketball team, if they hadn't known before, knew now.

But Zack only smirked. "What's up, Liz? Jake not keeping you happy? I mean, if you're feeling unsure, I can always, y' know, reorient you—"

"Fuck you," Liz spat. "Why the hell do you have the right to tell her who she can love? Is it really any of your business?"

"Chill out, Liz," Zack said. His lip was curling up in a

sneer, and it was not an attractive look. "Listen, I'm just trying to do the right thing here. God hates fags, right?"

"I don't think God hates anyone," Kennie said very quietly from behind them.

There was a small silence, and until that moment, Liz had been rather neutral on the whole gayness thing. But as she stared at Veronica standing in the corner with her hair in her eyes and half the basketball team around her, Liz realized that though she didn't know what was right, she knew that what Zack was doing was wrong.

"C'mon, *assholes*," Zack said, smirking, and slowly the boys followed him, though not without throwing a number of dirty looks at Liz, not without muttering and laughing as they walked away. Kennie asked Veronica if she was okay, but in a distant sort of way, because they were from different social castes and this exchange broke a number of rules. Liz turned for the door, and Kennie followed after a moment, and they never spoke of it again.

The next day, Liz sat at lunch and someone made a homophobic joke and Liz gave the punch line—"Because God hates fags"—and they all laughed. She didn't meet Kennie's eyes, and when the laughter died and the conversation changed direction, Liz looked at the next table, where Zack sat with his group of friends.

I'm not one bit better, am I?

CHAPTER FIFTY-FIVE
What Liz Also Didn't Know

*L*iam had seen the entire thing.

He had driven back to school because he had left his phone in his locker, and on his way through the gym lobby, he saw Liz Emerson snapping at Zack Hayes, and it was an immensely satisfying sight.

It struck him that perhaps she thought just as many thoughts in a minute as he did, felt just as many emotions, inhaled and exhaled just as he did. And it was then that he began to fall in love with her for the second time, for the same reason that he had picked up his flute again: because he believed in broken things.

And I know it isn't his fault, not really, but I wish he would have told her. I wish he had told her.

CHAPTER FIFTY-SIX

The First Visitor

*L*iz is being moved out of the ICU and into a private room. Monica cries when she hears the news. Julia wipes at her nose surreptitiously. Kennie bawls. Liam overhears and closes his eyes, and quietly thanks everything that will listen.

One visitor at a time, they are told. But the fact that they are allowed to visit at all is such an improvement that they can't help but hope.

The room is cold and dim and unfriendly, and Liz looks like hell. When Monica sees her, she feels such a strange mix of elation and sadness that her breath turns heavy and she almost cannot go on, but she does. She goes to Liz's bed and looks down at her daughter, and she wonders what her husband would have said if he were here.

"Elizabeth Michelle Emerson," she whispers, stroking Liz's hair away from her face. She remembers being just two floors above here, holding Liz when she was still just a small bundle of pink in her arms. She remembers shifting Liz from one arm to the other so that she and her husband could sign the birth certificate beneath the name that they had chosen so carefully.

Through her tears, she says softly, "Please don't make me write it on a tombstone."

I hover at the edges of the room and echo.

Please.

Please.

Please.

SNAPSHOT: FUNERAL

Her hair lies in damp curls on the nape of her neck. Her hands are streaked with dirt. The mud makes squelching noises between her toes when she walks.

We are very solemn as Liz buries the worm found lying dead in the driveway.

She kneels in the rain-soaked grass and lays the worm in the dirt. Her nose is running, and I am hugging her fiercely.

She cannot bear to catch fireflies in jars. She hates zoos. She will not let her father teach her about constellations, because she will not trap the stars. She lives in a world made entirely of sky.

It is inconceivable that one day, her world will grow so dark and distant that when she raises her head, she will not be able to find it.

CHAPTER FIFTY-SEVEN

The Last Day of Liz Emerson's Childhood

On the day Liz's father tried to fix their roof but died before he could, Liz and I drew pictures of ourselves on the roof with chalk. On that day, her hair was tucked into a blue wool hat and I wore the dress Monica wouldn't let her buy. There was an impossibly blue sky above us, and after a while, we realized that the day was too perfect to be spent drawing pictures. Liz gathered the chalk back into the box, and we began playing tag.

Our laughter floated into the sky. We were happy, and the world was wide.

"Be careful," Liz's father called.

We tried, we really did. But the wind asked us to dance.

The loose snow took our hands and twirled us around. The cold was everywhere, but so was the sun, and it was irresistible. It made us reckless and invincible, and after a minute, we forgot. Liz chased me and I ran a little too close to the edge.

I wobbled.

She screamed.

Liz's father spun around too quickly, and lost his balance.

And Liz screamed some more.

A neighbor came to investigate. She called the police and got Liz off the roof. Later there was a funeral and a fatherless family, and Liz had to be pried off the coffin, finger by finger.

She never stopped blaming herself.

CHAPTER FIFTY-EIGHT
Hickeys and Black Eyes

Jake Derrick finally arrives in the waiting room.

He walks over to where Kennie and Julia sit and says, "Hey."

Kennie ignores him entirely.

Julia looks up. She gets slowly to her feet and says, "Jake."

"How is she?" he asks.

Julia examines the hickey on his neck. "Where have you been?"

He runs a hand through his hair. It's so overly gelled that the crinkle fills the room—the junior class has paused its card games to listen. "I didn't hear about it until an hour ago," he pleads.

"You were in school today," Julia says flatly. "It was all

over Facebook last night. You couldn't have *not* known."

"Oh, come on," he says, growing defensive and consequently unpleasant. "You know I was at basketball practice last night. And I don't check my wall every five minutes, like some people."

Julia's eyes narrow. For a moment, her expression is so uncannily similar to the one Liz often wears that Jake is unnerved. "Nice hickey," says Julia. "Who was it?"

"I don't—"

"Your girlfriend," Julia says, "is fucking *dying.*"

That shuts him up, because Julia never swears.

Jake collapses into a chair and rubs his face. He looks tired, afraid, and I know that he cares. But like Julia, like Kennie, I hate him because he has never, ever cared enough.

"I didn't know what to do," he says in a hollow voice. "I heard that she was in the hospital, and—god, Julia. We had a fight on Sunday, okay? I tried to apologize and she told me to go away. Do you know how guilty I've been feeling? God, don't you think I regret all the things I said to her?"

Julia stares at him for a moment. Then, without warning, she punches him in the face so hard that his chair falls backward.

And with Jake curled on the floor, shocked and wincing, his hands cupped over his eye, Julia says in a hard voice, "This is not about you."

CHAPTER FIFTY-NINE
The Second Visitor

*I*n the commotion, no one notices that Liam gets up, shoves his hands in his pockets, and walks after Monica.

He arrives just as she is leaving Liz's room.

"Oh," she says, hastily wiping at her eyes. "Hello. You . . . are you . . ."

"May I see her?" he asks quietly.

She hesitates, considers him as she has never considered any of Liz's boyfriends, and gives a small nod.

Liam has to close his eyes for a moment, because she looks so, so much like Liz.

Then he reaches for the door, his fingers curling around the cold handle, takes a breath, and goes in.

He leaves the door open and feels Monica standing just out of view, giving him a privacy that he is grateful for beyond words. He doesn't want to be quite alone with Liz Emerson, but he wants to see her. He wants to see her.

He sits in the chair and looks at her. Carefully. He follows the tubes running up her nose and taped to the insides of her wrists. He observes the infinitesimal rise and fall of her chest. He can see the faint blue of her veins beneath her gray skin.

He says one word.

"Why?"

It's something that he has wanted to ask her for so long that hearing it aloud is strangely surreal. He wanted to ask her at the end of fifth grade. *Why haven't you noticed me?* He wanted to ask her during freshman year. *Why did you do it?* He wanted to ask her when he watched her staring at the sky. *Why are you afraid of being yourself?* He wanted to ask her that day in the gym lobby. *Why do you want to be unbreakable?* He wanted to ask her after the party. *Why don't you remember?*

He never asked before because he didn't think she would answer.

She doesn't.

"Liz," he says, and that's another thing that he's always wanted to say, her name. Just her name. "Liz, I never thought you'd be the first one to quit."

He grips the metal bars on the side of the hospital bed until his fingers are nearly as white as her face. "Liz," he says. He closes his eyes and leans his forehead against the bars.

"Please," he whispers. "Remember the sky."

She doesn't respond, and after another minute, he leaves.

CHAPTER SIXTY

Two Days Before Liz Emerson Crashed Her Car

"Ms. Emerson," Ms. Greenberg said severely. "Why aren't you working?"

"Forgot my calculator," said Liz.

It was a combination of her careless tone and her incomplete homework and the fact that she had forgotten her calculator every day for the past week that led to Ms. Greenberg's ten-minute lecture on the irresponsibility of today's youth, and at its conclusion, Liz was sent to her locker to retrieve her calculator.

Liz's locker, however, was on the second floor and on the opposite side of the school, and she was too lazy to walk that far. Since Julia's locker was conveniently located down the hall, Liz decided to borrow her calculator instead.

When she spun the lock and opened it, however, it was not the calculator that caught her eye.

There was a ziplock bag sticking out of Julia's backpack.

Liz swore and grabbed it, looking around to make sure she was alone. She shoved it deep in her purse, slammed Julia's locker shut, and walked back to class.

She didn't even realize that she had forgotten the calculator until Ms. Greenberg demanded where it was.

"I couldn't find it," Liz snapped, and Ms. Greenberg gave her a detention for Friday afternoon for "blatant disregard for the tools of mathematics."

Liz threw the detention slip away as soon as she left precalc, because she didn't intend to be alive on Friday afternoon.

She headed straight back to Julia's locker. As she walked closer, she could see Julia rummaging around frantically, searching.

"Hey," said Liz. "Here."

Julia snatched the bag, her gaze flashing around to make sure that their exchange had gone unnoticed. "Why did you—"

"I came to borrow your calculator," Liz said, "and found *that*. Are you *stupid*? God. The drug dogs could have come today. Any fucking teacher could have opened your locker and found it—"

"Seeing as my locker was *locked*," Julia said, "I don't think that would have been a problem. Give me my calculator back."

"I didn't take it," Liz snapped. "Damn it, Julia. Why do you even have it here? You *know* that you can't just—"

"I ran out, okay?" Julia said quietly. "I talked to Joshua Willis and he got me some. It isn't a big deal."

"It isn't—*the fuck it isn't a big deal*. You told Joshua Willis? Joshua Willis *knows*?"

"I told him I was getting it for a friend, okay? Chill. He'd never think it was for me."

But the words shook as they fell; Julia's entire body shook, and though she looked on the brink of tears, her voice was angry.

"I have to go to class," Julia said when Liz was speechless.

Liz watched her walk away, her heart pounding. God, if Julia were caught. She didn't know what Julia would do. She didn't know what *she* would do.

She went to chemistry, but she couldn't focus on the notes. The teacher lectured on stoichiometry, and at the end of the hour, Liz still didn't know what the hell stoichiometry was. She hurried down to Julia's locker and caught Julia just as she was leaving, and when Liz called her name, Julia stiffened.

"We're going to be late," Julia said.

"Julia," Liz pleaded, "please tell me you gave it back to Joshua."

Julia said nothing.

"Give it back to him," Liz said.

"Don't tell me what to do."

"Please," Liz said. "Please, Julia."

"Liz," Julia said, and her voice cracked. "I can't."

"Jules," she said, but Julia had already disappeared into the swarming crowd of students. Liz leaned against the lockers and was suddenly frightened, because she was losing Julia. And despite the fact that in two days she would lose everyone, she wanted Julia to be okay. Julia was cracking, and Liz just wanted to keep her from falling apart, because in her heart, Liz Emerson knew that she was the one who had put the cracks there in the first place.

Liz attempted to talk to Julia after government, searched for her in the halls when that failed, but Julia avoided her deftly. Because they were not in the same lunch, Liz tried to forget it and listen to Kennie chatter, but everything around her was fog and white noise.

Finally the last bell rang, and Liz caught Julia on her way out of the building. For a few seconds, they walked in silence; then Julia pushed the doors open and a blast of frigid air hit Liz in the face and slapped the words from her mouth, words she'd held back since the first moment she had realized that Julia was addicted.

"Julia," said Liz. "You need to get help."

Julia spun around. "Shut up," she said, and walked away.

Liz kept pace with her, her teeth carving into her bottom lip as she tried to find the right thing to say. "Julia, please," she said. "Go see a doctor or something. We can keep rehab a secret. Please. God, Jules, you're going to ruin your life if this goes on—"

"Me?" Julia's voice was so hard that it stopped Liz in her tracks. "I didn't ruin my life, Liz. You did."

Liz stood there for a long time, trapped between those little words and the truth of them.

I'm sorry.

Those were the right words. She just hadn't been able to get them out.

Liz stumbled back against the side of the school and leaned her forehead against the cold brick. The rough surface stuck to her skin, and when she closed her eyes, the tears froze on her eyelashes.

Julia was right.

It wasn't just people Liz disliked that she destroyed. It wasn't just nerds, or gays, or sluts, or band geeks, or the members of the crappy cheerleading team, or the chess team members, or the Buddhist Club members, or the quiet ones, or the annoyingly loud ones that Liz destroyed.

She destroyed everyone. Even the people closest to her. Especially the people closest to her.

And even when Julia texted her that night to apologize, saying that she didn't mean it, that she was just PMSing, even when Julia made it clear that she was willing to forget, there was no going back.

Some people died because the world did not deserve them.

Liz Emerson, on the other hand, did not deserve the world.

CHAPTER SIXTY-ONE

World of Idiots

"*O*h my god," Kennie says in a teary, wavering voice. "You hit him."

Julia says, "I think I should have aimed lower."

Kennie sniffles. "I wanted to hit him too," she says, and begins crying again.

Julia sighs and puts her arms around her. "What now?"

"She's going to kill me," Kennie says with a muffled wail.

"Why?" Julia asks. Because honestly, there could be a number of reasons. All the crying, for example. Liz hates crying.

"Because," Kennie sobs, "I didn't get it on video."

Julia stares at her.

Suddenly they're both laughing, and it's a relief. They're laughing as hard as they were crying, and everyone is staring, and for once, neither of them cares. And there are so many things to laugh about—they've done so many stupid things. They are a group of idiots in a world of idiots, and Liz was the most idiotic of them all.

Finally, when they calm down and wipe away the laughing tears as well as the sad ones, Kennie stands up, wobbly.

"Where are you going?" asks Julia.

"To get a picture."

CHAPTER SIXTY-TWO

The Third Visitor

*J*ulia gets up too. Monica is standing guard by the door to Liz's room, but she gives Julia a hug and a shaky smile, and walks away. Julia goes in. There's a nurse wearing scrubs with pink dinosaurs, adjusting one of Liz's tubes.

"How is she?" Julia asks.

The nurse turns and smiles at her, and Julia can see in her eyes that she's considering a lie. But in the end, the nurse says, "Honey, she is an absolute mess. But she's holding on."

Julia can't help it. She begins to cry. She rubs her eyes furiously because everyone is crying, and honestly, she's sick of it. She sees why Liz hates it so much.

The nurse gives her a sad smile and leaves, and Julia sits down in the chair that Liam vacated moments before. She touches one of Liz's hands, and it's so cold that a tremor runs through Julia. Liz always had cold hands. Bad circulation. Julia takes Liz's fingers in hers, careful to avoid the needles and tubes, and tries to rub some warmth into them.

But Julia's hands are cold too, as she stares at Liz's quiet face. There were many days when Liz was strangely, inexplicably quiet, but not like this. There were many parties at which she had found Liz crying, but they had never really talked about why. Behind all of her wildness and anger and insanity, Liz was a girl of silence, and Julia always let her keep her secrets.

Now Julia wonders exactly how many secrets Liz had.

Julia didn't drink at that first party.

She didn't like the smell of beer, and she was already drunk on the fact that they were there at all. Kennie was curious, but not, at that point, enough to try it.

Liz, on the other hand, celebrated by forgetting everything she had ever learned in health class. She had three Solo cups of beer and was completely wasted.

Near one in the morning, when Kennie's brother arrived

to pick them up—having been paid fifty bucks to keep all of their parents ignorant of their whereabouts—Julia realized Liz was missing.

She found her upstairs, in bed with Zack Hayes, and he was trying to get Liz's shirt off.

Liz was trying to say no, but she was too drunk to get the word out.

Zack leaped off the bed when Julia entered, and Julia, after getting over her initial shock, decided that the best thing to do was to get Liz out of there. She dragged Liz down the stairs to find Kennie pushed against the wall, wrapped around some senior whose hands were already at her shirt buttons. Julia grabbed her too, and she pulled them out into the night.

Something changed that night. Liz was different after that.

That night, Liz's self-respect began to chip away, and then she had let it fall, piece by piece.

I think Julia is beginning to realize this. She remembers what the doctor told Monica yesterday, what Monica told her, what she told Kennie, and what Kennie told everyone else: that Liz will only pull through this if she's determined to.

The nurse escorts her back to the waiting room. She had

run into Liz's room after hearing a crash, and she found Julia beside an overturned chair, shaking.

Julia doesn't struggle. She's held silent by the overwhelming fear that Liz Emerson, her best friend and the most obstinate person she knows, no longer wants to fight.

CHAPTER SIXTY-THREE

The Maternity Ward

*K*ennie wanders around the hospital until she finds Jake seeking comfort with a young, pretty, overly sympathetic nurse. She hears a bit of what he's saying as she walks closer, "something real" and "in love" and "lost without her." She thinks about hitting him again, or maybe kicking him this time, but in the end, she doesn't. She takes a picture of his brilliantly purpling eye, flips him off, and starts back to the waiting room.

Unfortunately, Kennie's sense of direction is virtually nonexistent, and within a minute, she is hopelessly lost.

She sees an elevator and heads for it. She begins hitting buttons, figuring one of them will take her back to the emergency room. None of them do. She passes the pediatric ward, the cancer ward.

And then she finds herself at the maternity ward.

She steps out of the elevator. She hears the faint, thin wails of babies, and her hands go automatically to her stomach. The flatness makes her throat close, and all she wants is to sit and curl around herself, around the baby who is no longer inside her.

On the day of their junior homecoming, the humidity was at 100 percent.

Liz didn't bother trying to curl her hair. Julia helped her stack it all atop her head while Kennie struggled with the iron and the hair spray, and when they were finally dressed and ready, they went to the beach to take pictures.

Jake was drunk when he showed up, and their pictures showed it. Liz told him not to drive and he told her to relax and then to fuck off, and by then she was pissed enough to let him go.

He arrived in one piece, though, and they grinded for maybe two songs before Jake disappeared, and Liz grabbed another boy and wondered why she was surprised. A scavenger hunt, a *yes*—did she really expect that to mean that Jake would change? People never changed.

She went to get a drink and hovered by the door to the gym for a moment, watching. There was a wall of heat there, and it smelled like the boys' locker room. The floor was damp with sweat, and when she finally went back in and grabbed Thomas Bane's hand, his shirt was so wet that it stuck to his torso.

She didn't care. She danced and danced and closed her eyes, and when the DJ announced the end and the lights came on again, she grabbed Julia and Kennie so they could go party.

They didn't, however, end up going anywhere.

Instead, they sat in the school parking lot inside Liz's Mercedes and listed off the things they knew.

First, that Kyle Jordan would break up with Kennie if he found out. Kyle had colleges considering him for tennis scholarships and he would never jeopardize that, and he was an asshole besides. They wouldn't tell him, because he would have dumped Kennie for much less.

Second, that they would keep it a secret. No one but Kennie, Liz, and Julia would ever know. Liz would get Kennie whatever she needed. Kennie must never, ever tell her parents. They would kill her. They would literally throw her out on the streets.

Third, that Kennie had to get rid of the baby.

"Wait," Kennie said into the silence. "What?"

"Kennie," said Liz, staring ahead into the dark parking lot, "you can't keep the baby. You know that."

Kennie curled over, her arms wrapped around her middle, her head on her knees.

"Liz," she said, trying to keep the tremor from her voice.

Liz ignored her. "We'll get you an appointment as soon as possible. Before it's too late. How long have you known?"

"Liz."

"*Damn it*, Kennie. God, if you ran out of condoms, why didn't you go buy some? You live a freaking mile from the gas station. It would have taken two seconds. Damn it all. You could have asked either of us. God, Kennie. I have birth control in my fucking purse. God. Whatever. It doesn't matter. We'll get rid of it."

CHAPTER SIXTY-FOUR

Fourteen Minutes Before Liz Emerson
Crashed Her Car

Liz got back onto the interstate after her single detour. She wiped her eyes and thought of Newton's Third Law. Equal and opposite reactions. That was the one she had struggled with the most. Moving objects, not moving objects, force and mass and acceleration—she had been able to puzzle those out, mostly. But for their unit on Newton's Third Law, the law of action and reaction, Mr. Eliezer put hyperlinks and videos on his website and told them to just go for it. It was supposed to teach them critical thinking and twenty-first-century skills and time management and other useless crap.

Naturally, most of the class sat on the countertops and shot rubber bands at each other.

Liz liked being in control, and she had the necessary leadership—manipulation—skills, but she was also a bit lazy. She never did today what she could do tomorrow, and she always believed herself when she used *eventually* as an excuse.

This inevitably led to late-night cramming sessions, which was exactly where she found herself the night before the test on Newton's third law. Unfortunately, Mr. Eliezer decided to surprise them with an essay test instead of multiple choice.

Liz's conclusion had read: NEWTON WAS A SPECTACULAR MAN AND MR. ELIEZER, I'D REALLY, REALLY APPRECIATE A D ON THIS TEST.

He gave her a D minus and a warning to study for exams. Liz had promised that she would, because at the time, she'd had every intention of doing so, eventually. But soon after, things began to slip downhill very quickly, and Liz gave up. The week before exams was her last week ever; she knew exactly which day she would get out of bed and never return, and her promise to study Newton the virgin felt more distant than a dream.

She knew it was stupid to try to understand now, since there were an infinite number of things she would never understand, so why should Newton's Third Law of Motion matter more than any of those? She, Liz Emerson, was going to cease to exist in mere minutes, and everything she knew would disappear. It didn't matter at all, what she did or did not understand.

She started thinking about all of the things she had done, all of the horrible things she had set in motion, and she wondered why none of them seemed to have had equal and opposite reactions. She thought about Julia's addiction and Kennie's baby and Liam's sadness and all of those other people she had kicked to pieces, and she thought about how she was never caught. Never. She was never punished for any of it. She had never gotten a suspension or an expulsion or a deportation, though she probably deserved all of them.

Liz Emerson had dished out a lot of sadness in her short and catastrophic life, and no one had ever done anything about it.

She did not realize that the equal and opposite reaction was this: every terrible, horrible, bitchy thing Liz had ever done had bounced back to her.

CHAPTER SIXTY-FIVE

All These Impossible Things

*K*ennie had always been happy as a follower—a good thing, because she had always been a follower. She had grown so used to following that when the topic of abortion came up, Kennie almost agreed without considering what *she* wanted.

There was, of course, the fact that Liz was right. God, her parents would disown her. She would never go to college. All of Meridian—half of which went to her church and would think of her during every single sermon about fornication—would give her dirty looks for the rest of her miserable, collegeless, homeless, parentless, unequivocally suckish life.

After Liz dropped her off, Kennie went inside, cried so hard that she puked, and somehow made herself believe that it was morning sickness, never mind that she was only about six weeks in. She took a shower and then suddenly it was all very real to her, this pregnancy. When the purple positive sign first appeared on the test, her heart had fallen out of her chest, but she had told herself that it was a hoax and ignored it. When her period never came, she finally told Liz and Julia, and now, Kennie put her hands on her stomach and believed for the first time that there could be a person inside her.

So sometime between shampooing and conditioning, she stopped being stupid and started falling in love.

It was kind of amazing, that there was something inside her, alive, breathing in and out—metaphorically, of course—and growing with each moment. It was very precious to her, suddenly, life. She had never valued it as much as she did then.

She wanted to keep the baby.

Kennie had always loved babies.

She had never taken care of anything before. Her parents were the definition of overprotective, and where they did not interfere, her brother did. Kennie had grown up so safe and sheltered and spoiled that she had learned little during her life except how to lie—a necessary skill if she wanted to have the barest semblance of privacy. In her heart, Kennie was younger than Liz or Julia, and she didn't like it.

In the shower that night, Kennie cried harder than she had ever cried before. She cried until the shower was icy rain all around her, because she wanted impossible things.

After her mother pounded on the bathroom door, demanding what was taking so long, Kennie came out, got dressed, and stayed up all night.

She sat in the darkness and tried to sort out her options. She put her hands on her stomach and hugged the growing life inside her, and tried to find a path wide enough for both of them.

She had $639.34 left in her savings account from her summer job at McCrap's. That might cover a month in one of those really disgusting apartments by the highway. Of course, her parents had guardianship over her bank account, and they'd probably lock her out of it.

She could call her brother, but he was halfway across the country now, and it didn't seem likely that he would help her. Never mind how many babies *his* girlfriends had probably aborted—he would side with their parents.

Maybe she could stay with Liz or Julia. But she'd still be in Meridian and people would still find out. Of course, she wouldn't even have to stay with Liz or Julia unless her parents kicked her out, and her parents wouldn't kick her out unless they knew she was pregnant, and if they found out, they'd tell the entire town anyway. She was going in circles.

Around three o'clock, she ran out of tears and decided to stop thinking about what to do.

Instead she thought about the baby.

My baby, she thought.

She didn't care about the gender. An hour later, she had names picked out for both, perfect names. She wanted to buy baby clothes. She wanted a car seat. She wanted a future that she could build all by herself.

But when she curled up beneath the covers and listened to her breath bouncing off her blankets, she began crying again because she knew she couldn't do it, not really, not ever.

She couldn't.

CHAPTER SIXTY-SIX
Thirteen Minutes Before Liz Emerson Crashed Her Car

*L*iz fumbled to get her phone out of her back pocket. The car swerved a bit, and her breath caught. A strange thing rose in her chest; she didn't know if it was fear or anticipation, but then it burst and she was hollow again.

She unlocked her phone and opened Facebook, and scrolled through her pictures until she found the one she was searching for. It was from the summer before eighth grade, and the three of them stood with the state fair in the background. Julia was wearing a pair of sunglasses she had just bought from the vendor behind them, and Kennie was holding a dish of deep-fried pickles.

That was the last time they ever went to the fair, though

Kennie brought the pickles up on a regular basis as a not-so-subtle hint. The appeal of carnival games and rides beneath an open sky had disappeared.

In the picture, Julia was still beautiful and brilliant and fully alive. Clear too, without the poison leaking out at the edges. And Kennie. She was laughing, of course, laughing like she used to—so loudly that an echo reached Liz through all the years and secrets and mistakes. God, how long had it been since she had heard Kennie laugh like that?

This was the *before* picture, and it broke Liz's heart.

Liz stared at her phone. She wanted to go back. She wanted to be a little girl again, the one who thought getting high meant being pushed on the swings and pain was falling off her bike.

I want to go back.

I wanted her to come back too.

CHAPTER SIXTY-SEVEN
The Abortion Clinic

Silence in the Mercedes.

And then.

"Want me to go with you?" asked Liz.

Kennie bit her lip. Her eyes were closed, but Liz could see her eyelashes glimmering with the tears she was trying so hard to hold back. Kennie wasn't wearing any makeup. Liz couldn't remember the last time she had seen Kennie without makeup.

Liz couldn't stand it. She leaned forward and hugged her tight, and tried to swallow the lump in her own throat. "Hey," she said, but her voice was a plea. "It'll be okay. Okay?"

Kennie nodded against her shoulder but said nothing. She got out of the car.

Liz sat in the parking lot alone. There it was, the silence again. It grew and pounded until at last she moved, savagely, jammed the keys into the ignition and backed up with a squeal. She drove down the street to the gas station, where she grabbed a pack of condoms, slapped it on the counter, and dared the cashier to comment.

She went back to the clinic, and when Kennie came out, Liz gave her the condoms. Kennie stared at them.

"I can't," she said. "Not for a month, at least. I'll tell Kyle I'm on my period."

For a month? Liz wanted to say. She didn't. "Just in case."

Kennie closed the condoms in her fist. She shoved them in her purse and didn't look at Liz.

And only then, when it was too late, Liz wondered if she'd made a mistake. *Here,* she'd wanted to say. *You still have Kyle. You have us.*

Liz dropped Kennie off and watched her walk into the house, and she began to cry. She cried as she drove, and she didn't care that she couldn't see the road.

You still have me.

The worst part of being forgotten, I think, is watching.

I watched her cry. There had been silent tears and ones

that barely leaked out. There were tears that heaved from her in great sobs. They all slipped through my fingers when I tried to catch them, and they fell around her in oceans.

I watched her carve her mistakes in stone, and they arranged themselves around her. They became a maze with walls that reached the sky. Because she learned from so few of them, she was lost. Because she didn't have faith in anything, she didn't try to find a way out.

I watched her try to face her fears alone, too proud to ask for help, too stubborn to admit she was afraid, too small to fight them, too tired to fly away.

I watched Liz grow up.

You still have me.

CHAPTER SIXTY-EIGHT

One Day Before Liz Emerson Crashed Her Car

*A*fter lunch, they had a Random Pep Assembly.

Their principal had established RPAs—because that was actually *what they were called*—last year to "boost student morale," the lack of which became the official excuse as to why Meridian's test scores had failed to meet state standards yet again. No one complained because it meant shorter classes and an afternoon of doing nothing.

Today, the teachers would have a free-throw competition, and the Future Farmers of America (a club that Liz often ridiculed) held a fund-raiser for their spring trip to the World Dairy Expo (seriously, they made it too easy), letting students buy votes to nominate a teacher to kiss a pig. They raised more than two thousand dollars.

Liz remembered why she used to like school. It was an escape from her enormous, silent house. School was always noisy, filled to the brim with different and irritating people. But between sophomore year and junior year, she began to want to escape school too, because now the hallways were filled with people she had torn apart.

On her way to the gym, she saw Lauren Melbrook. After she, Julia, and Kennie had spray-painted SLUT across her front lawn, Lauren had kind of faded. Liz knew that she used to be part of that Ralph Lauren sweater-set group, but of course they had pushed her away after the pictures made their way around Facebook. There were rumors that Lauren was now on heroin, and though Liz knew that she shouldn't put too much faith in gossip, Lauren was indeed walking with a group of verifiable dealers.

Liz took her seat in the front with the other kids who went to the right parties and wore the right clothes and kissed the right people, but as she sat, she caught sight of Sandra Garrison's round stomach. She had gotten pregnant about a year after the pregnancy and abortion rumors had made the rounds. Since everyone thought Sandra had already been pregnant once, she figured that she might as well live up to expectations. She was a senior now, but no way was she going to college. A pity—she had been on her way to being valedictorian.

And there was Justin Strayes, sitting alone at the edge of the bleachers. His GPA had nose-dived after the drug dog incident, and now he was on the brink of failing every single one of his classes. And he had been voted Most Likely to Succeed at the end of eighth grade.

A cheer erupted from the gym floor—Mr. Eliezer had just won the free-throw contest. The girls around her were screaming their heads off, because Mr. Eliezer was the youngest teacher in the school, and *hot*.

Kennie was on the floor with the dance team, Julia was waiting to sing with the rest of the show choir, and even Jake was on the sidelines, waiting to give a speech for the student government.

Liz felt very small after spotting each of them. Everyone around her was just bursting with talent—except perhaps Jake, who, for the sake of the nation, she hoped would never be allowed to have anything to do with the government. Still, even Jake was funny and almost smart, and once he grew up a bit, Liz thought that he could make someone happy. Maybe.

In that moment, Liz Emerson felt that she was forever looking up at people who were much, much better than she ever could be, and the only thing she was really good at was pulling them down to her level.

A part of her couldn't help but hope that she simply hadn't found what she was meant for yet, so when the assembly ended and everyone headed for the parking lot, Liz slipped through the crowd and headed to the guidance counselor's office.

Yesterday, she had told Julia to get help. Here was a chance for her to not be a hypocrite, and surely she owed it to herself to take it.

Liz was reluctant because she and her counselor had had a deep and unspoken hatred for each other ever since she had blown up in his office last year, after he had tried to impress upon her that she simply didn't have the intellect to take AP classes and refused to change her schedule to accommodate the classes she wanted to take.

Still, she went to the guidance office and knocked on the door. She had nothing to lose. Mr. Dickson—his name was a testament to his stupidity; in Liz's opinion, a man with the last name *Dick*son should have had the self-respect to not work in a high school—was sitting on his chair, his butt hanging off both sides, and it was with some difficulty that he turned around. His face fell a bit when he saw Liz, but he waved her in all the same.

"Liz," he said in an overly cheerful voice. "How can I help you?"

Liz hesitated. The words were there—*I need help*—but

her tongue would not support them. Her lungs would not force them out.

"I have a problem," she finally said.

"What kind of problem?" he asked, immediately wary. "Do you want to change your schedule for second semester?"

"No," Liz said, and then she stopped. She knew that she needed to tell someone that she was suffocating, but she didn't want that someone to be Mr. Dickson.

Very slowly she said, "I think that I might be slightly depressed."

"Oh," Mr. Dickson said, sounding nervous. He pushed his glasses up his nose. Liz wondered if any student had ever come to him for actual guidance before. Under any other circumstances, she wouldn't have either.

"Well," he said, "perhaps you should see a psychiatrist, Liz. I can't suggest any treatment—"

You can't do jack shit.

"—but what do you think is bringing you down, exactly? We can talk about it, if you'd like."

Liz picked at her nails. Her manicure was chipping, and she watched as little pieces of her glittery blue nail polish flaked off and drifted onto her jeans. "I dunno," she said at last. "I guess . . . I guess I've just made a lot of mistakes."

Mr. Dickson leaned back in his chair. "Well," he said, "I think that may be a good thing. You see, Liz, we learn from our mistakes, and the more we make, the more wisdom we gather over the years—"

"Yeah, okay, I don't need any of your Dr. Phil crap," said Liz, and she hated herself, because maybe, maybe Mr. Dickson truly wanted to help her. She just didn't know how to stop. She had been on autopilot for too long.

Mr. Dickson's expression hardened. "All right, then, Liz. What do you want me to say?"

"I don't know," she snapped. "Aren't you supposed to know what to say?"

"Ms. Emerson, I can't help you if you don't want to be helped."

But she did want to be helped. She just didn't know how to ask for it, and she was very much afraid that she was beyond any kind of help, regardless.

Mr. Dickson sighed. "You know, Liz, I also went through a dark period during my youth. I've always been a bit overweight—"

It took every single ounce of Liz's self-control to keep her mouth shut.

"—and for a while, I was very conscious of what others thought of me. But I *overcame* that," he said, leaning forward. The chair creaked. "I began to see that it simply didn't matter what others thought, that it was what I thought of myself that mattered most—"

Okay, Liz thought. *Screw this seven chances thing. Just kill me now.*

"Just remember, Liz," Mr. Dickson said, "it's never too late to change. Every day is a blank page, and your story has yet to be written."

Liz laughed. It was a breathless, desperate sound. "Oh, I think it's too late, Mr. Dickson."

He smiled at her kindly. "Well, Liz, you'll never change if you don't believe you will."

His words hit her physically. Liz forced a smile, and then she left. Outside, it was between winter twilight and nighttime, a dusky compromise that was not quite one thing or another. Liz ran across the parking lot, and when she reached her car, she leaned her forehead against the side. Her skin stuck to the metal, and all around her, the sky was darkening.

"Well," she whispered, "I guess I can't change, then."

CHAPTER SIXTY-NINE
The Fourth Visitor

Mr. Eliezer had seen her brightness right away, even though she kept it suppressed and boxed in. She had asked enough intelligent questions between her asinine ones, and even on the first day, he had seen that she could have been a brilliant student if only she would apply herself. That, he had learned, was the worst part of teaching: seeing students give up before they even started.

He had badgered Liz more than any other student, because he had never seen a girl so filled with could-haves.

Mr. Eliezer doesn't stay for long. Monica is still guarding the door—she'd been reluctant to let him in at all to leave his card. He smiles wanly at Liz, as though she can see, and walks out.

The card reads: DEAR MS. EMERSON, YOU SOLEMNLY SWORE THAT YOU WOULD RAISE YOUR GRADE IN MY CLASS, AND THIS OATH REMAINS YET UNFULFILLED. GET BETTER.

CHAPTER SEVENTY
One Step Forward

*S*ince Liam never really went to parties, he became addicted to caffeine instead of other stuff. The cup of coffee that Monica brought him had tasted like plastic, but he needs a refill or he'll collapse. The stress has gotten to him, and right now he really wants to sleep, but he wants to wait for Liz Emerson more.

Liam happens to really like hospitals. His mother is a nurse, and a good part of his childhood had been spent in sterilized hallways. This has always been a place of miracles, not death, and he'd like it to stay this way.

A nurse tells him that there's a café on the fifth floor when he asks, but when he gets in the elevator, he accidentally hits the button for the fourth. He sighs and rubs his face, unreasonably annoyed that the elevator will hesitate on the fourth floor, but there's nothing he can do about that now. He presses the right button, leans back, and closes his eyes.

He actually falls asleep for a second like that, standing, his arms crossed over his chest. Then the elevator opens on the fourth floor, and sobbing jerks him rudely from his momentary oblivion.

He blinks. By the time he is truly awake, the elevator doors are already closing. He blocks them with his arm and steps toward the girl slumped in a corner of the hall.

Liam looks down at Kennie. He hesitates, but after a moment, he clears his throat.

"Julia?" It's a hopeless little thing, her voice, and skeptical. Surely she must know he isn't Julia. *Not even she's that stupid,* he thinks as he crouches down by her. "Jules, is she better?"

"She got moved to a room," Liam says. "So yes."

Her head snaps up, and Liam really looks at Kennie for the first time. The truth is, Liam has always thought of Kennie as a slutty, stereotypical Barbie with even less intelligence. Because that's what he's been told.

Now he looks at the grimy tracks of makeup on her cheeks and the broken girl trapped in her eyes, and he realizes that he's an asshole.

He realizes, suddenly, that all humans are, well, *human*.

"You aren't Julia," she says.

"No," he agrees.

She sniffles. "Liam, right?"

There, there it is. Before his eyes, Kennie transforms back into the girl everyone expects her to be, slightly idiotic and slightly above the rest, because that's what they've made her.

Liam decides to let it go. Kennie is lost and terrified. He won't let her be alone too.

Everyone wears masks, Liam decides. He's no different.

He offers her a hand. He says, "C'mon. You want to see her?"

Kennie hesitates.

But in the end, she takes his hand.

CHAPTER SEVENTY-ONE

The Night Before Liz Emerson Crashed Her Car

Liz sat in her closet and cried. She cried and cried and hated the world and cried, and by the time she stopped, she was empty. Because there was no one to hate but herself.

Oh, she was still angry with others, for reasons that she knew were wrong. She was angry at her mother for not caring and she was angry at Julia for not being strong enough and she was angry at Kennie for being such a fucking idiot and she was angry at Liam because he had made it possible for her to destroy his life and she was angry at Jake for being an asshole and she was angry at all the people she ever hurt because they just sat there and let her, let her run them over until there was nothing else in her way.

Sitting in her closet, she thought about how this was the last time she would ever sit in her closet again. It was a strange thought. She dug her fingertips into carpet and leaned her head against the wall and thought, *Never again.* There was no going back. The next morning, she would go to school and face one last day, just one, and she would look around and everything would be exactly the same, and people would treat her the same as ever. They would talk and laugh and complain about homework and make fun of teachers, and only she would know that there would be no future. Tomorrow, everything, everything would end.

And god, it surprised her, how desperate she was for it.

She took out her phone and Googled "signs of suicide."

Deep sadness.

Loss of interest/withdrawal.

Trouble sleeping or eating.

Having a "death wish," taking unnecessary risks such as driving over the speed limit, running red lights, etc., being excessively reckless.

Increasing use of alcohol or drugs.

Mood swings.

Oh. Well.

No one noticed?

Come on. Trouble sleeping—the irony.

Seriously.

Really?

Her resolve turned from cement to steel. Because no one noticed. Anything.

The section below gave tips on overcoming depression and suicidal thoughts. Liz didn't read them.

There was no getting better.

Not for her.

CHAPTER SEVENTY-TWO

The Day Liz Emerson Crashed Her Car

She tried to enjoy it. She tried to tell herself that she still had this last chance, these last few hours to find a reason to live, but she was numb. She wanted it to end.

She saw Julia laughing before government, but there were shadows under her eyes and a tremor in her fingers. She saw Kennie dancing through the hall, but there was something forced about her laughter. She sat in physics as Mr. Eliezer reviewed Newton's laws of motion for the exam, but she didn't understand a lot of it and thought to herself, *Doesn't matter.*

When I crash, I will be inertia mass acceleration force gravity opposite equal everything.

I will be nothing.

When the final bell rang, Mr. Eliezer kept her after class to ask why she hadn't turned in her physics project yet. She didn't say much, but still, by the time he let her go, the halls were mostly empty. She put her textbooks in her backpack and dug her keys out of her purse, and as she walked downstairs and turned for the doors, she saw something that made her stop.

It was Kennie. She had changed into her dance uniform. Her forehead was against her locker, her arms were wrapped around her stomach, and even from where Liz stood, she could see that she was crying.

Liz walked out, started her car, and drove to the gas station. She filled her tank with enough gas to get her to her destination, and then turned in the direction of the interstate.

CHAPTER SEVENTY-THREE
Seven Minutes Before Liz Emerson Crashed Her Car

She finally figured out that she, Liz Emerson, was the equal and opposite reaction. She was the consequence.

She pushed down on the gas pedal.

CHAPTER SEVENTY-FOUR

The Fifth Visitor

*L*iam leaves Kennie by Liz's open door, and Kennie goes in slowly. The light is dim. Liz's hands are by her sides and she's wearing a hideous hospital gown, and this is how Kennie has always imagined bodies inside a coffin.

Kennie sits down beside the bed and does what she does best. She talks.

"So," she says, "I was upstairs in the maternity ward. They are so freaking adorable. The babies, I mean. You know, I've always wanted a sister. Like, one Christmas, when I was four, I wrote to Santa and asked him to exchange Daniel for a big sister instead. Brothers are just kind of useless, you know? You can't borrow dresses or shoes from them or anything."

Kennie stops. The quietness makes her eyes water. But Kennie isn't just Liz's small, shallow, idiotic, perky, bouncy friend with an immense talent for bawling her eyes out. In that moment, she proves it to herself.

"Yeah. Well, Jules has your math homework. I would have taken chem notes for you, but we didn't take any. Or that's what Jessica Harley said. I skipped class. I heard that everyone just kind of sat there. You would have hated it. I mean, if you had been there, we probably wouldn't have had to sit around all day . . . never mind. You have to get better soon, or else Jake's face is going to heal and you'll never get to see his black eye. It's fantastic. Julia hit him pretty hard. He actually fell backward. Maybe you can give him another one. Oh my god, that would be so great! He'd be like a panda! Hey, by the way, are the two of you even still together? He said you had a fight or something. No one knows what's going on, Liz. I hope you guys are broken up. I hope you don't get back together with him. Liz, you're too good for him."

Kennie pauses, glances at the doorway, and then gives Liz a conspiratorial look. It's what she would have done if Liz was awake, but it's disconcerting, Liz's stillness, her closed eyes. Kennie makes herself go on, but the lump in her throat turns her voice into something unfamiliar. "You know Liam? I mean, I know he's kind of a nerd, and we were kinda total bitches to him freshman year. But he's kind of cute, don't you think? He has nice eyes. And, fine—he totally likes you, Liz. He watches you, like, all the time in school. I can't believe you haven't noticed before. It's totally cute—not creepy at all. Maybe *watches* isn't the right word, then. But he pays attention, Liz. And he's, like, smart too. Remember when he won the spelling bee in fourth grade? Wait, you weren't here yet. Well, he won the spelling bee in fourth grade. You guys will make such a great couple. I'm just saying. You have to get better soon so you can make out with him and tell us about it, 'kay?"

That's when her voice breaks. The crack starts at her throat and stretches all throughout her, and Kennie's grip on herself begins to slip. "You have to get better soon," she says. "Liz, just come back. We'll get your car fixed. We can hold all of your notes and homework and stuff for you. We'll fix everything, okay?"

She swallows hard. She leans her cheek against the railing and looks at Liz's face, and whispers, "I'm sorry I was so mad at you. I know it wasn't your fault, with the—the baby. I . . . I'm going to break up with Kyle. And Julia . . . I don't know if she already told you or not, but she said to me earlier that if you got better, she'd tell someone. A rehab person or something. Liz, it'll be okay. It'll all be okay."

Kennie blinks as rapidly as her sticky, mascara-y lashes will allow. She wipes her eyes quickly with the back of her hand. "Sorry. I'm not crying. Not crying. Okay, remember at the end of, like, seventh grade when I got those stupid matching rings for us, and we swore to be friends forever? I still have mine, you know. And Julia has hers. And I know yours is in the bottom of your jewelry box. I saw it there when I borrowed that one necklace for homecoming. Oh, hey, I still have that, by the way. Remind me to give it back to you. Anyway . . . Liz, forever means, like, *forever.* As in, you can't just leave us behind. Liz—"

A small sob rises in her throat and lodges there, and it takes all of her strength to choke out the next words. "Liz, you have to pull through this. You have to. You can't leave us behind. We—we can't do this without you. God, Liz. Please."

Then Kennie begins to cry, because no one is strong enough to hold back so many tears.

CHAPTER SEVENTY-FIVE

The Worst Part

*L*iz never got to say her good-byes.

Julia left that day while Liz was still talking to Mr. Eliezer. The last time Liz saw her was in the hallway. She had been on her way to Spanish, and Julia had been going to gym. Julia hadn't seen her—she had been too busy trying to pull her ridiculously long hair into a bun, and part of Liz knew that it would be the last time. They had no other classes together, nor any classes that would make their paths cross, and so when she saw Julia, she stopped in the middle of the hallway and just watched, trying to impress that moment into her memory, never mind that her memories would cease to exist in mere hours.

Later, when Liz had seen Kennie crying by her locker, she had wanted, so much, to go and put her arms around her. But Liz knew she would let something slip. Kennie knew her too well. She would suspect. So Liz had turned and walked away.

Her mother, of course, was flying home, but as Liz drove out of the parking lot, she called her anyway. The call went straight to voicemail, but she listened to her mother's voice one last time. She wanted to say sorry. She had so many things to be sorry for. Instead, she hung up.

But in the end, she took only one detour. On her way to the crash site, twenty minutes from the end, Liz turned onto an exit ramp and drove to the state park.

She didn't get out, only stared at the very tip of the scenic tower peeking over the trees. She thought of all the wishes she had made up there. She thought of her father racing her to the top, letting her win. She remembered how desperately she had once loved the sky, and finally she said those two small words that had been fighting to reach the air for so long now.

"I'm sorry."

CHAPTER SEVENTY-SIX

And Then Things Fall Apart

*K*ennie is still there when the beeping begins.

Soon there are doctors and nurses rushing into the room, saying things that Kennie doesn't understand, and she's sobbing because something terrible is happening and she doesn't know what.

The nurse with the pink dinosaurs takes Kennie's hand and pulls her out of the way.

"What's happening?" Kennie sobs, hysterical. "What's going on?"

The nurse folds Kennie into her arms and says, "Oh, honey. Her heart is failing again. It . . . it doesn't look good."

"No," Kennie blubbers, fighting out of the nurse's grip. "It isn't true. Liz!" she screams. "Liz, you are not fucking doing this to us. *You will pull through this.* Liz. *Liz!*"

CHAPTER SEVENTY-SEVEN

Two Minutes Before Liz Emerson Crashed Her Car

She remembered me.

She remembered the little girl she once was, the one who believed in magic and love and heroes, the one who held funerals for worms she found dried out on the driveway. She remembered a time when she was happy and the world was bright, and she remembered the imaginary friend she once had.

Since this was the end anyway, she imagined that I was in her passenger seat. She imagined that my hand was over hers, that it was warm over her cold one, that it was holding hers steady.

In those last moments, she was not alone.

CHAPTER SEVENTY-EIGHT
Voices

"Someone get Dr. Sampson on the phone. Tell him that her pulse is erratic—"

"What happened? She was fine a second ago—"

"Well, she isn't now, is she? Get that blood—he must have overlooked something, something's hemorrhaging—"

"Oh, for the love of god, get her out of here!"

Someone takes Kennie by the arms and drags her away.

CHAPTER SEVENTY-NINE

The Crash

*F*or the last time, Liz Emerson wished to fly. There were no snowflakes or dandelion seeds this time, but as she closed her eyes and jerked on the wheel, she made her wish.

She did not fly.

She fell.

She thought, *Hello, gravity*, and tried to spread her arms so that it would catch her.

Hello, good-bye.

But the world did not fade completely.

CHAPTER EIGHTY
Silence

"What's going on?" Monica flies out of her chair, and the room erupts as three male nurses drag Kennie into the waiting room. Julia looks up. Her heart drops through her body and keeps going.

One of the nurses pulls Monica aside and tells her what has happened. The rest of the room is quiet, watching, and when they see Monica's face crumple, they hug each other and grab tissues and begin to cry.

Except Kennie. Kennie goes to Julia and grips her hand with all her might.

CHAPTER EIGHTY-ONE

Before Everything Fades

Mr. Eliezer concluded their review on Newton's laws of motion like this:

"Right. Remember, all of Newton's laws are about the theory of motion. In this class, we're assuming that friction, air resistance, and all other factors are negligible, but very rarely can Newton's laws be wholly applied in the real world. Things just aren't that simple."

And when the class had yet again expressed its indignation that they were studying something that couldn't even be applied, Mr. Eliezer just smiled and said, "There's more to life than cause and effect."

Things just weren't that simple.

In that moment, everything *clicked*.

And Liz Emerson closed her eyes.

CHAPTER EIGHTY-TWO

The Waiting Room Again

*T*he nurses hurry back to Liz's room. Monica comes over and puts her arms around Kennie, and Julia holds her hand as though she never means to let go.

The rest of them watch. They wait for an ending. They wait for a world where Liz Emerson does not exist.

Jake Derrick sits quietly in a corner, his head in his hands. Of course, he had been sitting like that ever since the hot nurse had left and people had started pointing at his black eye, but when the news about Liz came, his head dropped a little lower.

Matthew Derringer goes outside and reorders the flowers he had canceled earlier.

Liam sits frozen, steam drifting up from his coffee.

Then, suddenly, Kennie raises her head. Her hair is twisted and tangled around her shoulders, her cheeks are black from her mascara, her eyes are red. She scans the room and finds Liam, and she says his name.

Liam turns his head warily, the entire room watching him.

Kennie doesn't break his gaze.

After a small eternity, Liam gets slowly to his feet. He takes silent, measured steps to Kennie, and for a moment he only looks at her, this small girl who has the potential to be so cruel but holds just as much sadness as he does.

He takes her hand.

Julia takes his other hand. He glances at her, and she manages a very small smile through her tears. Monica gives him a look that makes him forget how awkward he feels to be holding hands with two of the most popular girls in their grade.

They stand there in that tight, bizarre circle, all thinking the same thing.

If she's determined to pull through this, she will.

I sit behind the brown couch where she left me, holding snapshots.

Her, pretending to fly, her arms wide as she runs through the park, my hand in hers. The fairy dust she tossed over me lifts my feet ever so slightly off the ground.

Her, making snow angels. Two of them, so that we can lie side by side, our wings touching.

Her, chasing me through the backyard, the summer grass warm beneath our bare feet.

Her, forgetting.

Me, watching all of the years go by.

Then the silence of the big house is broken by the crunch

of car tires pulling into the driveway. I hear the garage door open with a mechanical whir, and then a turning lock.

"Careful," Monica says. "Watch your crutches."

The answer is an automatic one. "I'm fine, Mom."

There is a pause, a small silence.

Then Monica says, "Honey. Do you need help?"

Another pause.

Then, very, very quietly, Liz Emerson says one word.

"Yes."

If you or someone you know needs help, resources are available 24/7, including the National Suicide Prevention Lifeline (1-800-273-TALK (8255) or www.suicidepreventionlifeline.org) and the Crisis Text Line (text LISTEN to 741-741).